WARRIORS IN THE CROSSFIRE

WARRIORS
IN THE CROSSFIRE

Nancy Bo Flood

LJCDS —

In peace —

find that inner
warrior!

Nancy Bo Flood

BOYDS MILLS PRESS
Honesdale, Pennsylvania

Copyright © 2010 by Nancy Bo Flood
All rights reserved
For information about permission to reproduce selections from this book,
please contact permissions@highlights.com.
Designed by Helen Robinson
Printed in the United States of America
First edition

Library of Congress Cataloging-in-Publication Data

Warriors in the crossfire / Nancy Bo Flood. — 1st ed.
p. cm.
Summary: Twelve-year-old Joseph helps his family to survive when the natives
of Saipan are caught in the crossfire between the Japanese soldiers and the
American troops at the end of World War II.
ISBN: 978-1-59078-661-1 (hardcover : alk. paper)
1. Chamorro (Micronesian people)—Northern Mariana Islands—Saipan—History—
20th century—Juvenile fiction. 2. Saipan—History—20th century—Juvenile fiction.
3. Saipan, Battle of, Northern Mariana Islands, 1944—Juvenile fiction.
4. World War, 1939-1945—Northern Mariana Islands—Saipan—Juvenile fiction.
[1. Chamorro (Micronesian people)—Fiction. 2. Saipan—History—20th
century—Fiction. 3. Saipan, Battle of, Northern Mariana Islands, 1944—Fiction.
4. World War, 1939-1945—Northern Mariana Islands—Saipan—Fiction.
5. Survival—Fiction.] I. Title.
PZ7.F6618War 2010
[Fic]—dc22
2010007095

Boyds Mills Press, Inc.
815 Church Street
Honesdale, Pennsylvania 18431

10 9 8 7 6 5 4

For Felipe I Ruak, Reilighmun, Keeper of the Dance,
his wife and family,
and for Bill, with whom I dance

WITH GRATITUDE

"I fell to my knees and wept." Frank J. Bohac, Lieutenant, 4th Marine Division, World War II.

My father fell to his knees and wept along with hundreds of his comrades on a tiny beach on Maui, Hawaii. In a few days his military orders would have taken him to the shores of Japan. His predicted survival time? 36 seconds. His orders? Kill everything that moved—man, woman, or child.

He fell to his knees when he heard the announcement: the war was over. Japan had surrendered. August 14, 1945.

I thank the universe that the invasion of Japan did not happen.

I thank the people who lived through those horrific times and continued to hope, rebuild and forgive. To all the people who shared their stories, the Carolinians, Repagúnúworh (Rapaganor) and Refaluwasch (Rafalawash), the Chamorro of Saipan and Guam, the veterans from both the American and Japanese armies, thank you. And the people who loved them, their wives and children, who hoped for their safe return. May your stories light a candle for peace.

I thank those who helped me create a story of peace out of war: Nancy Weil; Kim Stephens; my family (each of you!); Veni Folta (kanji consultant); Vermont College of Fine Arts faculty Marion Dane Bauer and Julie Larios; and all you Whirligigs, Cookies, and Plateau Authors. And thanks to Carolyn Coman and Jane Resh Thomas from the Highlights Whole Novel Retreat—you asked the hard questions and encouraged me to continue. I thank my editors at Front Street–Boyds Mills Press—Erin Garrow and Joy Neaves—and Kent Brown, publisher, for believing in this story.

Thank you.
Nancy Bo Flood
Chinle, AZ

WARRIORS IN THE CROSSFIRE

I did not know
My people's blood would turn the ocean red.
I did not know
Night's quiet would become my enemy.
I did not know

"They're coming. Get down. Now!" I stared into the darkness at the black curved beach. Soldiers should not have been patrolling so early. The last group usually finished their round at midnight. Waves lapped against the wet sand. Palm fronds clattered. I heard the sounds of hard leather military boots stomping across loose coral and rock.

"I don't see anything, Joseph." Kento stepped closer. He studied the dark stretch of sand. Then he squeezed my arm as I pointed to four distant silhouettes.

I used the silent hand signals we had practiced. Kento nodded and stepped backwards, crouching low beneath branches of young coconut palms, then scooting his legs into the tangled bush and vines. We lay motionless in the sand.

Voices. They *were* early. The patrol usually made its first round of the day long after dawn ... after we would have been far out at sea. But the dark sky above us showed no sign of the first morning light. This must be a new night patrol.

Stay facedown! Don't move! I signaled.

"But the rats, Joseph."

"Rats bite, Kento. Bullets kill. Stay down."

Already I could hear a man speaking—gruff Japanese words that I could barely understand. The soldiers laughed. Kento would understand. His father spoke only Japanese to him. But I didn't dare ask him what the soldier had said. My heart pounded so loud I thought they'd hear it, look down, and see us—two boys hiding in the shadows—one a villager, and one the son of a Japanese official.

I hid my face in the sand and clenched my jaw. *I don't exist, son of a Saipan chief, hiding in the sand.* The soldiers walked past and continued to the far end of the beach. Their voices faded. Finally the only sounds remaining were the splashing waves and the clattering palm fronds.

I looked up. Kento still lay facedown in the sand. I touched his arm, and he turned to face me. We exchanged glances—a quick rise and fall of the eyebrows.

Ready?

Yes. I am ready.

Soon, I signaled. Today's hunt would be our test. As warriors we could help our families survive—*if war comes*—the words we often thought but never spoke out loud.

A ghost crab scuttled past my nose and tiptoed side-ways, its stilt legs barely touching the sand. I turned my head. Startled, the crab darted back into its hole. Sand fleas bit my ankles. Others feasted on the line of sweat across my neck. We didn't move or make a sound. The Japanese patrol would walk to the end of this beach, past the end of our village, and shine their searchlights across the tumble of volcanic boulders until, satisfied that no enemy soldiers—no Americans—were in sight, they would turn and walk back. One last time past us.

We waited. The smell of cigarette smoke drifted our way. They, too, were breaking the rules. More guffaws. The new night patrol was almost over.

When the soldiers were a dozen strides past us, I pushed myself up to see more clearly. A branch snapped. The soldiers jumped like frightened minnows. Searchlights blinked on. Silver beams sliced across the shore and pierced the tangle of branches. A dark shape burst from underneath a nearby bush and dashed across the sand. A shout. *Crack!* A gunshot shattered the quiet. Light beams stretched and stopped. A dead rat lay in the pool of silver light. One man grunted; another laughed. Then silence.

Search beams again crisscrossed over the beach. More laughter. Nervous and brief. The lights clicked off. The soldiers walked back up the beach. Gone.

"Joseph, that was so stupid." Kento hissed the last word, almost spitting in my face.

I looked up and down the empty beach. "We'd better go."

Kento stood glaring, shaking his head.

I looked away and then again scanned the beach. "We leave when you are ready."

"I am ready," he said. "A samurai warrior is always ready."

"Good. Let's begin."

海龟 鲛 TURTLE AND SHARK

Avert your gaze,
Do not see
Fear.

We retrieved my outrigger from its hiding place in the bushes and carried it to the water's edge. Kento and I waded on opposite sides, guiding the craft away from jutting rocks and chunks of coral. Once afloat, the canoe glided silently across the surface. When the water reached our chests, I nodded to Kento. He hoisted himself in while I steadied the canoe. Too much weight on one side and the outrigger would flip. Kento had tipped many times, learning how to land low and centered. I had tried to be a patient teacher, as my father had been for me, righting the outrigger again and again, until he could board without causing a ripple.

"Good. Lie flat along the bottom. Remember, stay out of sight. An island warrior stays invisible."

Kento's eyebrows arched. "Invisible? What about silent?" He slid flat into the bottom of the canoe.

One last look down the beach. The soldiers' lights were gone. I gave the outrigger a shove, rolled in, and paddled hard for the *ava*, the narrow cut in the reef where the sea rushed out of the lagoon as high tide changed to low.

I guided the outrigger between coral heads, waited for a big wave to lift us, and then paddled hard, working with the outflowing current. We flew up, over the outer edge of the reef, and were free. Free of the rules, the restrictions, the always watching, patrolling soldiers. The Japanese may have taken our stores, our schools, even our lands, but they could not take this. Not the ocean.

Outside the lagoon, the ocean deepened. Below us, shifting shadows of indigo and black disappeared into the depths. Knowing that this rippling surface continued deeper and darker into the western edge of the sky made me shiver. What lay beyond that straight-line horizon? When would I sail that far, like my uncle, one of the greatest navigators of the Pacific?

"Is this where we hunt?"

I had forgotten about Kento. He still lay flat in the canoe, his face pale. "No, not here, Kento. The turtles sleep in undersea coral caves on a shelf off to the south." I breathed in the cool, salty air. "It's safe to sit up now. The warships are way north. We can't be seen by soldiers patrolling on shore ... or by my father." I grinned.

The island lay far behind us, and the eastern sky was already streaked with blushes of early dawn. "We need to finish the hunt and return before anyone notices. Remember, if anyone asks, we spent the morning hunting octopus, not out here past the reef in the forbidden sea."

Kento still lay stretched out flat along the canoe's bottom. I lifted my paddle, paused, then slapped it against the next wave. *Whoosh!* A shower of cold water splashed over the canoe.

Kento sat up, sputtering. "Joseph!" The canoe wobbled. He gripped the sides. "When we get back to shore—" We both broke out laughing.

I raised my paddle, threatened another splash but stopped. "Kento, this is important: as soon as you spear the turtle, I'll help you pull it up into the canoe because sharks will smell its blood." I circled my hands closer and closer toward Kento. "If that happens   *bam!* Grab a paddle and smack it in the nose."

"But Joseph—"

"What?"

"I am not a strong swimmer, and ..."

"And what?"

Kento looked down. "I hate deep water."

"You will be in the canoe, not in the sea." I rested the paddle across my knees. "Kento, you don't have to do this." He looked scared. "You are the only one who knows if you are ready."

Kento's hands shook. "I must become a warrior, Joseph, an island warrior as well as a samurai. For my family, if they need food."

I nodded. "The first time my father took me over the reef to spear fish, a shark brushed across my thigh. I wanted to climb onto the reef and stay there. The sea was as dark as octopus spit. But my father tied the first fish to my waist and said, 'Fear is a good teacher.' After that my eyes never left the water. Another shark began circling. Its fin cut through the waves. Father punched hard at its nose and, like that,"—I snapped my fingers—"the shark was gone. We caught over twenty fish that night. Half of them hung bleeding from my waist."

I turned back around and picked up my paddle. "See, Kento, the eastern rim of the sky is brightening. We need to be floating over the coral shelves before it gets any lighter."

I paddled with a steady rhythm ... raise, dip, pull, lift ... soothed by the repetition, the splashless dip of the paddle, the pull of my arm, the glide of the canoe. We passed over a series of coral heads, and I gazed down to watch the shifting colors and shapes. In this first light of morning, the giant globes shimmered like pearls. Black-and-white-striped fish swarmed over the glowing heads, then scattered in an instant as the dark shape of the canoe passed overhead. Schools of flying fish leaped alongside us, skimming the surface in unison like slender silver birds. I watched for parrot fish: brilliantly colored sentinels that guard their underwater territory with their large white teeth. They would be emerging from their night cocoons.

"Take a look, Kento. The ocean is ours."

Kento peered over the edge, then pulled back. "The canoe might tip, Joseph."

I laughed. "Don't worry. The sea is calm. Everything quiets at dawn. The wind, the waves, even the ocean." But Kento sat like a stone in the middle of the canoe.

"Fear is good unless it grows too big. Then it is more dangerous than spilled blood." I echoed my father's words: "Face your fear; sail through it." I remembered from my first turtle hunt areas of dark, endlessly deep ocean. I did not admit to Kento that, even today, I steered the outrigger away from those dark, unreadable depths.

Dawn was spilling light across the waves. Blood-red streaks cut along the wide straight horizon, separating ocean and sky. I set down my paddle, cupped my hands into the water, and splashed myself and the canoe. The beginning of a new day and the beginning of a new hunt—both were sacred. It was time for a warrior to give thanks. "Spirits of the sea, let us travel safely across your back. We give you honor and ask for your protection." I repeated my father's prayer, words of respect. "We hunt for the Old Ones; we hunt with humility and to bring food to our families. Guide us with gentle winds. Help us to return home safely."

Wings pulsed overhead. "Look, Kento. Fairy terns. A good sign." A pair of slender white birds circled wider and higher. Their shrill cries called *Follow us!* I smiled. Yes, a very good omen. Perhaps they brought the sea spirits' blessings. The pair soared in synchrony, one a pale shadow of the other. They would fly across the open ocean, farther than I had ever paddled, fill their gullets with fish, and return to feed their young ones nested in the cliffs above our village. I shook my head. If war really did come, what would happen to them? Where would they hide? What would happen to us if those soldiers, patrolling every beach, marching on every street, had to fight, to defend?

The current pulled stronger now, sweeping us away from the island, far from the reef. The gray, hulking warships looked small and far away, not even real. The shimmering surface of the ocean rippled around us.

The sun climbed, brightening the high ridge that ran like a green arched backbone the length of the island. It rose over Mount Tapotchau, the highest point and the island's center, and daylight poured across the sea. Cool ocean spray splashed my face as I paddled into the waves. Sunlight warmed my back. The rhythm of the waves quieted my thoughts.

These first shafts of light now pierced the deep water. Turtles would soon stir, feel the need for air, and start their swim upward. Our hunt would begin.

I sat upright, scanning. A submerged cluster of coral caves lay a few paddle lengths below our canoe. Carefully I set the paddle against the canoe's side and whispered, "Kento, it's time. Watch the surface for a round shadow. Or the tip of a beak. Signal when you see something."

On my first hunt my father explained that in early morning the Old Ones' eyes are blinded by the low morning light. All night the turtles sleep in these undersea caves where they are safe. They rest, not breathing. At dawn their need for air forces them to the surface.

With the grace of great seabirds, the turtles glide upward, using their flippers like wings. "Watch for a dark beak breaking the surface," my father had instructed. "Drift close until you can see the nostrils flare open. Stay soundless. Hide in the sun's shadow. The low morning light blinds them, but respect their strength and sharp jaws. One snap and you can lose your hand. Focus on their weakness, their blindness." I did not want to admit even to myself that I wished my father were here now to guide us. He would laugh, perhaps dive in and ride one of the big ones, holding onto its shell while splashing through the waves. It was strange to be beyond the reef without him. I looked back. Our island felt far away.

"Kento, be ready. We will drift with our backs to the sun so we are hidden in the sunlight. The turtle will not see us until it is too late."

"I understand."

I shook out my arms and breathed deeply. Once Kento speared his turtle, I would dive in, take hold of its shell, and use all my strength to help lift it into the canoe. The sun was now above the high ridge of the island, igniting the waves. From our small canoe, the ocean was immense.

Kento sat straight and alert.

I whispered. "Relax. We are hunting turtles, not

sharks. Be careful not to bump against the canoe. The sound will warn any turtle and then it will surface somewhere else. The first turtle we see, he's yours. Ask permission to take him. Ask his spirit to give you his courage."

"You want me to talk to a turtle?" Kento looked at me, eyebrows raised and mouth open, but he said nothing more and picked up the spear.

"Good. Throw hard and straight." I nodded. "The way we practiced. Stare at the turtle. The throw of your hand will follow the focus of your eyes."

Kento slid his hand along the smooth wood of the spear until he got to its throat.

"Watch for the beak. When you can see the nostrils, drive the spear deep into the neck and hold onto it until I lift the turtle up to the canoe. Don't lean over the side. Don't tip the canoe." I dipped my paddle into the water and pulled, redirecting the canoe's course. "Ready?"

Kento nodded. His knuckles were white. On my first hunt my fingers became numb. I wasn't afraid of the turtle or the sharks but of falling into the sea and sinking too deep to ever swim back up. The sea had swallowed many men from our village.

Shapes appeared beneath the rippled surface. Shadows of fish darted by so fast I wasn't sure which were real and which imagined.

Kento pointed. A dark shape glided toward us. A hawksbill turtle bobbed to the surface just an arm's length away.

"Look at the size of its shell! It must be very old and strong." It was hard to only whisper; I wanted to shout, but the turtle would hear my voice and disappear. "This is a good omen, Kento. Wait, watch, then throw hard!"

The turtle drifted closer. Its hooked nose dipped upward, the nostrils flared open. A movement distracted my focus. Did I imagine the shadow following behind?

I blinked and looked again. There was nothing.

Kento raised his spear, ready to throw.

I saw it again. A dark gray shadow followed just below the surface. A fin sliced the water.

"Stop!"

Kento's spear flew fast and straight. Blood spurted. "I did it!" Kento yelled. In the same instant he lost his balance and fell forward. The canoe rocked.

"Don't move! Lie still." The outrigger tipped far to one side, then back to the other. Kento rolled, grabbed the edge, leaned against it to pull himself up.

"Stay down. Don't move."

"But the turtle—"

"No!"

Splash! Kento fell into the water. I grabbed for his arm. "Kento!"

He was gone, out of sight. A thin line of blood oozed toward the boat. "Kento!" As the dark water splashed and churned, my eyes searched. Where was the shark? The turtle? Where was Kento?

A dark head popped up. Kento windmilled with both

arms, spat, coughed, and gulped air, splashing wildly.

"Kick. Grab my hand." I reached as far as I could without tipping the canoe.

Kento clutched my fingers, then slipped and fell back. I stuck out the paddle. "Kick. Reach. Grab on!" But then I saw it again, the gray shadow, a fin, circling. "Behind you! Watch out! Punch it. Now, Kento, now!"

Kento turned but, like the turtle, was blinded by the sunlight.

I dove at the fin, my arms straight out, hands fisted. I struck. The shark turned and swam over me, pushing me down. It circled, ready to attack from above and sink its teeth into its prey. I punched blindly. It pushed me deeper. I kicked, not caring at what. The shark twisted away, then disappeared.

My lungs burned. The surface swirled far above. Below was blackness. An endless dark pit. I wanted to scream, to touch the light, but my eyes stung from the saltwater, and I began to sink. I pulled and kicked against the water, fighting to swim upward. The shimmer of light grew brighter. But far overhead. I kicked, struggled. My head broke above water, and I gulped sweet, wonderful air.

Kento was screaming. "Joseph, I can't swim much longer. I can't reach the boat." Where was he?

I twisted around and reached toward his voice. He grabbed onto my head and hung on, pulling me under. I yanked loose. "No. We'll both drown. Hold my shoulder and kick." Kento reached again. I could feel his weight, but as soon as he began kicking, we thrust forward. "Yes, that's right. Kick hard. We'll make it back."

Kento kicked. I pulled with my arms until we were alongside the canoe.

"Reach for the edge and hold on. Pull yourself up while I push from behind. When you can lean over the edge, kick and flip yourself in."

Kento landed with a *thunk*. The boat rocked, its sides slapping the water's surface. Kento began coughing, choking, vomiting water. I clung to the canoe and breathed, waiting for the strength to pull myself back into the canoe. "Kento, I'm coming in. Lean away. Don't let the canoe tip."

"Yes. I'm ready."

Once in the canoe, I began shaking—arms, legs, my whole body. I couldn't stop. Nausea filled me. I leaned over the side, threw up, then lay flat in the bottom of the canoe.

The sun slowly warmed my skin and chest, and finally the terrible chill deep inside me. The sea rocked the canoe, and the waves sang, slap-slapping against the sides. My breathing slowed. We were both alive.

I sat up. "You did it, Kento. You hunted turtle."

Kento sat slouched over, his head down. "My fear was too large. I nearly drowned us both."

"No. You hunted turtle."

"I am ashamed."

"You were afraid, but you did it. Someday we'll come back. The turtles will be here, and we'll come back."

Kento would not look at me. He stared at the horizon.

I picked up the paddle and turned the canoe around. "It's late. We need to get back before my father starts looking for me."

I paddled hard and fast. Kento stared ahead at the island. He said nothing until we were back over the reef skimming toward the cove. Then he whispered, "I apologize, Joseph. Thank you for saving my life."

I shook my head. "You have no reason to feel shame. The shark left quickly. My fist must have scared him." I tried to smile, but still saw the pit of dark sea that had been below me.

"When a samurai fails, he brings dishonor and shame to himself and his family. Shame is worse than death. That is our samurai code."

"You fought to survive, Kento. You fought like a warrior." I grew quiet. I had often felt shame, too. I knew words did not take away its sting.

The outrigger slid through the shallow water onto the beach. "Jump out and stay back in the trees. We'll talk tomorrow after school."

Kento leaped out, turned toward me, and bowed. "You are a true warrior. You risked your life to teach me your strength." He bowed again. A lone figure was walking toward us.

"Leave. Hurry!"

•

My father's straight back and steady stride were unmistakable. As always, he held his head high. He was tall and slight, unlike most of the village men who were wide-shouldered and broad-chested. They were men who could paddle a canoe all day without tiring or carry a bundle of coconuts for miles. My father, our village chief and clan leader, was not big, but he was quick and strong. When he led the warriors' dance, no one could leap as high or twist and strike as fast, and no one's eyes sparkled brighter.

Now his eyes were dark. I was in trouble. The new Japanese rules forbade us—any native—to use a canoe or fish outside the lagoon. We were all suspected of being spies, of sending information to the American military. We were not allowed to have a radio—none—in the entire village. No newspapers. Nothing printed. Each week brought new restrictions, earlier curfews, more arrests.

The closer my father approached, the faster my heart raced. I expected anything, even a blow. But my father's eyes showed only sadness. His face seemed tired. I stood straight, hands clenched, and did not look away.

He stepped closer. Flies whined around my ears, and my skin itched from the dried sea salt, but I did not move. Why didn't he say something? He stared, studying every inch of me.

"Joseph, have I taught you nothing?" He shook his head. "You risked your life and Kento's. You endangered both his family and ours. If you had been seen, you could have been arrested. All of us, our entire family, arrested and shot. Kento, too, his entire family—mother and father, even his sister, Ako, shot!"

I looked down, my heart pounding. A ghost crab tossed sand up out of its hole. Tiny shells moved as hermit crabs crept toward the tiny pools of water around my toes.

"Go home, Joseph. Your mother and sister need your help. Do not touch this canoe again." He turned and left.

I kicked at the sand. Seawater seeped into the crude pit, and I kicked again and stared at the reef. Surf leaped and crashed against the distant coral. The surf was not afraid—of soldiers or war or stupid rules—and I would not be, either. I had paddled over that reef. I closed my eyes and saw the flared nostrils, the hooked beak. I felt the darkness pulling me down, but I had fought for life and air and light. I would not fear war.

師 TEACHER

Young bamboo,
Bend.
Survive
Typhoon winds.

Next morning at dawn I hurried to Garapan, to school. The walk was long and hot, but I could not risk arriving after the final bell. I ran. The Japanese government allowed only a few native students to continue past the first three years of classes. I had been chosen as one of them. I would learn to speak proper Japanese even if they thought a native boy could only become a well-trained servant.

I had waited for Kento at our meeting place but he never showed up. Yesterday after the hunt I hadn't seen him—or my father—the rest of the day. Father had spent the afternoon at the *Uut*, the men's meetinghouse, discussing, arguing, debating the war ... all evening and into the night. My father sat cross-legged at the head post. Next year, once I turned fourteen, I would be expected to sit behind him and listen respectfully, never speaking. I was in no hurry to do that; I'd rather hunt octopus in the lagoon. The war talk was endless. Go ahead, Japanese and Americans, greedy bullies, battle it out and leave so we can have our island back.

A group of soldiers marched by. Something was different about them. These soldiers did not soften their grim, straight-ahead stares for an instant. Even the ones I knew did not nod or smile. They wore their usual full-legged, khaki uniforms. Another group approached, eight soldiers marching two by two. Each soldier carried a rifle. As they passed, pedestrians stepped back. Businessmen on bikes braked and stopped. There was no friendly chatter; no laughter came from women holding little ones and shopping baskets.

Where was Kento? He always knew the latest news about battles or maneuvers in the Pacific, information no one was supposed to know, especially me. His father was an administrator in a Japanese office in Garapan, at military headquarters. Recent reports were grim. The Japanese were losing important battles. The Americans were pushing the Imperial forces farther and farther back ... toward Japan ... toward us.

News and rumors spread by mouth faster than any wire could carry it. To be found with a forbidden radio or newspaper meant death by beheading. Or death for disobeying any of their rules which bite-by-bite had taken away our island, our way of life, like a shark tearing apart a turtle.

An eerie silence followed me as I rushed the last few blocks to school. Kento was not waiting by the school's front gate. I hurried through, past the oldest students, all Japanese, all neat and tidy in their white shirts and long pants. They frowned or ignored me, the unwelcome native.

Kento sat at his desk, practicing sums on his abacus. He would not look up. What was going on? I slid into my seat at the back of the room, last row, middle desk. The rest of the students hurried in with none of the usual teasing and joking. All faces were serious, eyes looking down. Our teacher, our Sensei, stood watching from behind his desk. Four soldiers entered. They stopped at the front of the room, turned and saluted Sensei.

We stood and bowed low.

The soldiers stood in a perfect, straight line, four khaki copies, each with a single bright gold star on his cap. Eight dark eyes stared straight ahead, hard as stone.

The first soldier stepped toward us, then spoke, "Sit down." We sat in unison. "Listen carefully. No interruptions. No questions."

No one even dared to breathe.

"By Imperial command, orders of the Divine Emperor, all schools on this island are closed."

I did not look up.

His clipped words continued. "You are to go home. Immediately."

I did not move.

The soldier turned to our gentle Sensei and saluted. "Report to military headquarters for further instructions."

Sensei bowed, eyes lowered, silent. I kept my own

head bowed, hoping my dark skin and wild hair would not be noticed. *Don't draw attention.*

The soldiers saluted, turned, and marched out. Their heavy black boots stomped on the cement floor. Gone. My ears hurt from listening. Outside a kingfisher squawked as if daring someone to shoot. Trade winds rattled through coconut branches, their tall slender palms swishing at the long rifles and gleaming bayonets.

Outside the school more orders were barked. Soldiers cried, "Great is our Emperor. Great are the Imperial forces. Invincible is Nippon, Japan, land of the Rising Sun. Victory forever!"

友達 FRIENDS

Rafalawash
And Rapaganor
Navigators from Satawal,
Pulawat, Yap,
Lamotreck,
Elato.
Warriors of the sea.

Sensei slapped a bamboo stick against his desk. "Be seated."

We sat.

"Listen carefully."

Slap! Another swift whack of bamboo against desk. "Gather your belongings, prepare to leave." Sensei looked away. His face looked tense and deeply sad. Another slap of bamboo, but this time a soft whack. Then a long pause. He coughed, cleared his throat, looked not at us but at some distant place. His next words were barely audible. "My students, go home. Speak to no one. Be careful, Kiotsu-ketsay, be careful. ... Obey." His final word felt like a heavy stone sinking into a dark, deep pool.

The older students bowed and exited. The rest of us scrambled to our feet and bowed in unison. Sensei returned our sign of respect and looked from face to face as we filed out.

I stared at the back of Kento's head, urging him to turn

around. Kento's mother is Rafalawash, from our clan. But his father is from Japan. He is the son of a Japanese citizen, and that makes all the difference between us. I am the son of a chief, a descendant of the ocean navigators of the islands Satawal, Pulawat, Lamotreck, Elato. But to the Japanese, we are all the same, we are natives, barbaric outsiders, *gai-jin*.

Why wouldn't he look at me? We have always been friends, even as little children. Japanese were never supposed to mix with natives, even before the soldiers patrolled the beach, but Kento and I were born in the same year, the same month, and our mothers are sisters. As kids we met every evening after chores at a tiny cove near our village. Fast as possible, I raced from our thatched hut to the beach, then headed north to the cove. There I dove into the warm, clear water and swam silent as a shark to the far side. Kento always waited there, having zigzagged down the rocky knoll from his cement-block house.

The cove was ours. Tucked inside an inlet that hugged a steep cliff, we caught ghost crabs and searched for smooth flat stones to skip. We wrestled, threw sticks at imaginary sea monsters, and when the sky became black, we flopped down on the wet, cool sand and stared at the stars.

Once, when we were small, Kento had said, "Someday, Joseph, I am going to Japan to study at a real university. Like my father. I will become an engineer and build an airplane that will fly to the moon. Maybe you can come with me."

"Maybe to the university, but not to the moon."

"Why not?"

"I will come back here and build a school. The finest in the Pacific."

"A school?"

"A school like yours. Then my people can learn everything. Like you do, but even more. Then this island will be ours again."

"Japan will not allow it."

"You will never go to the moon."

We wrestled again. Afterward we lay on our backs, breathing hard, not saying anything, knowing it was time to go home. We never spoke of it, but we never forgot—even for a moment—Kento is Japanese and I am not.

Someone coughed. Feet shuffled past. I had forgotten. Our school was closed. Forbidden to reopen until ... until when? Until it was too late for me? Kento hurried past. I raised my eyebrows. He hesitated, glanced at me, arched his eyebrows in reply. We would meet at Sa'dog Tasi, river to the sea, where the trees grow thick and tall—coconut palms, mango, and breadfruit, an impenetrable curtain of green. Within their safety, we would meet.

御法度 FORBIDDEN

This is not a game.

I slowed my steps. I would meet Kento, but I did not need to hurry. Sensei was the last to leave. He walked up to me, shook his head. Looking into my eyes, he said, "Joseph, remember. Think before you act; never give any dog reason to bite." Sensei's tall, thin frame looked frail and defeated as he bowed, then walked away.

I bowed farewell. Thoughts swirled in my mind.

I only wanted to learn the secrets of the Japanese—how to read kanji, the picture words, how to write the official papers to buy or sell land, how to send the abacus beads flying so I someday could demand: you must pay this much to grow your sugar cane on our land and use our water.

Alone in the courtyard, I hesitated, looked from wall to wall. Last week, I had struck Sato-san, a senior student. He and his friends had been laughing about the women in our clan, how they dress, wearing only a skirt. Sato-san insulted my sister, laughing and joking about how he saw "her ripe mangoes" as she walked from town. Sensei should have reported me to the police, but he had not.

Sensei had not sent me home. If he had, I would never have been allowed to return. Instead he gave me twenty-five lashes. I watched my blood drip onto the white coral-dust floor. I knew Sensei should have expelled me. He had the right to beat me as long as he chose, even to death. It had happened to native students at other Japanese schools.

"Hold out your arms. Hold them straight out." Sensei had placed a heavy brick on each palm. "Hold these this entire day. If you show anger at this school again, leave and never return."

Alone now in this courtyard, once again I held my arms out, looked at my empty hands, pressed them against the wall, and felt strong. Sensei had given me another chance. I would not fail him.

Then I began the hot walk toward home, but first to Sa'dog Tasi.

Kento whistled. This was our place, Sa'dog Tasi, river to the sea. Not much of a river now during the dry season, just a few inches of water meandering over a wide swept-out depression of white sand. But after a storm or typhoon, this river became a roiling torrent of mud-red rushing water.

I slipped into the tangle of vines, bushes, and trees. As my eyes adjusted to the dark shade, I saw Kento. He sat under a tall breadfruit tree, resting against the wide trunk.

"Why did they—"

Kento grabbed my arm and pulled me down. "Sh-h-h, Joseph, not so loud. Someone might hear you."

"The school, why did they close it?"

Kento glared. "Calm down or I'm leaving."

I glared back but didn't say anything. Instead, I threw stones at geckos that wiggled up and down the nearby trees. Finally I blurted out, "Are they going to kill us like they rounded up and killed the Koreans on Tinian?"

"Don't say such things! Do you have any brains inside that hard head?"

Talking about forbidden information was dangerous. If anyone heard us, we would be reported to the military, but I didn't care. I wanted some explanation, some answers. I nodded, then whispered, "My father was talking with the other chiefs. Some said that all natives— Rapaganor, Rafalawash, Chamorro—would be rounded up. Is that true? And the school, why was it closed?"

"Joseph. Open your eyes—the older students, the teachers, don't you see? More soldiers are needed. No more questions. We shouldn't even be here."

"No one will see us."

"We can't take any chances. Everything is different now."

"Different? What's different?" I looked straight at Kento. "You? Because of all this war talk?"

Kento looked away, but the muscles in his jaw kept working. He shook his head, whispered, "War is coming soon, Joseph."

I threw a rock against a distant tree. "War! Your Emperor uses war as an excuse to make us his slaves. 'Do this! Don't do that. Forbidden!' Everything. Soldiers come every day even before dawn and take our men, whoever looks strong, to the fields to cut sugarcane. All day. No pay. Nothing. Even my sister's husband, Ignacio, must go, and their son, Taeyo, is only a child. Who is going to fish? Climb the trees for breadfruit and coconut? Who?"

"That's why you must help me, Joseph. Many stores are being closed."

"What do you mean?"

"The soldiers use them to store guns and ammunition. Please, Joseph, teach me to be an island warrior, so I can protect my family and find food for them ... when ..."

"When what, Kento?"

"When the fighting begins—"

"Ha! What fighting!" I threw one rock after another.

"Joseph, we cannot meet here. Not anymore. No one must see us together, especially any soldiers. From now on we can meet only at night. At the cove. Like we did as kids. If I am suspected of anything, my family will suffer."

"Kento, you are talking crazy. Who cares about us? Anyway, I promise we won't go out past the lagoon again, over the reef."

"I must go now." Kento stood up. "This is not a game, Joseph. I am no longer a child. My father often does not return from headquarters for two or three days. My family needs me."

"Wait. I promise, no more questions." I shut my eyes, trying to shut out our words, trying to think.

Above us the strong branches of the breadfruit trees spread wide, a thick, safe canopy. These old, old trees had given us canoes and homes, food, protection from typhoons. Could they protect us from war?

Sensei says, obey. Kento says, give up your dreams and prepare for war. My father says, stay silent, wait. But I am Rafalwash, Rapaganor. The ocean is ours. This island is our home. No one can take them. No one.

"Kento, listen to me—"

My friend was gone.

友達 FRIEND

I miss the one
Who stares at the stars
And reaches
For the moon.

Kento and I did not see each other again for many days.
One long week passed, then another. Soldiers came to
our village and patrolled the shore even more frequently,
every few hours, day and night. They moved into our
church, slept on the benches, and cooked rice on the
altar. They took tins of tea, bottles of oil, and bags of rice
from our village store, replaced them with long boxes
of rifles and crates of ammunition, and stood guard at
the door. I spat into the coral dust when I walked past.
My fingers longed to throw the stones I carried in my
pockets, but I remembered the crack of the branch, the
gunshot, the silver pool of light, the dead rat.

I hurried past.

Then, despite rumors that dozens of Japanese planes
had been shot down by the Americans and that their
white-faced soldiers were hungry to eat our children, the
Emperor ordered a victory celebration.

Officials commanded the men and women from our

village to perform. All morning and into the afternoon we danced, first the women, then the men—our sacred warrior dances. I stayed near my father, pleased to be almost as tall, almost as strong.

I had learned from my father the ancient words of the chants and the ancient movements—the leaping, twisting, striking stick against stick. Gleaming with sweat and coconut oil, we danced, beating the rhythm faster and louder. Slapping, whirling, chanting our battle cries, we called to our ancestors. *Guide us! Give us strength to leap, to fly, to defeat our enemies.*

The Japanese sat in straight-row chairs, the men in starched white shirts and long white pants, the women in pale flowing dresses and sun hats, parasols perched above like colorful blossoms hiding their faces. They stayed distant and separate from us, but to each other they smiled, bowing and chirping like sparrows fussing over seeds.

Politely, they watched, laughing and applauding after each dance, understanding none of it. Except for one person.

Sensei sat near the other Japanese but off to one side. He did not laugh. He watched with respect, honoring the sacredness.

Behind Sensei sat Todaka-san, chief military marshal of the island. He had beheaded my mother's uncle, an old navigator and one of our chiefs. Todaka-san had commanded him to bow and obey or face death. He had chosen death. Kento had scorned the old navigator's disobedience as foolishness. For Kento, obedience is honor.

Kento and I had not spoken since Sa'dog Tasi. All this week his gaze had followed me as I gathered coconuts or breadfruit. At night, when I walked alone along the lagoon, I had felt his eyes. I knew he was watching the dances.

Why do you watch me, Kento Tanaka? Are you still my friend? Or is it true that your father spies on us?

As a lead dancer, I stood with the younger boys, guiding them, glad our dancing was nearly done. Sweat ran down my face, chest, and back. I raised my dancing stick, my warrior spear, and shouted in Rafalawash, "We are strong! We fight to defend our clan, defeat our enemies!"

Usually when my father danced, he laughed and joked, urging us to dance faster, sing louder. He would leap high into the air, twisting and spinning, sweat flying from his wild black hair. But not tonight. Tonight his mouth stayed shut in a grim straight line.

All day the soldiers had been celebrating, drinking too much sake, too much beer. They shouted vile words at us. I knew what their shouts meant. I glanced at my father ... *let us strike back.* His glare needed no words. I tried to close my mind to everything but the dance.

A group of drunken seniors from school pushed closer, taunting and laughing. Sato-san pointed at me. "Hey, naked dancer, where is that pretty sister of yours?"

Think only of the dance. Only a few minutes and we would be done. I could escape and return home. My hand tightened around my warrior stick.

"Hey, I'm talking to you. Bow, native boy. Bow to me!" Sato jeered.

I did not look at him. I did not answer.

"Your sister, so pretty, so naked—where is she?"

I stepped away from the dance and tried to slip into the crowd.

Sato stood in my way. "Where is she?" He held his cupped hands in front of him, grinning. "With breasts as round as melons?"

His drunken friends pushed closer, swaying and hooting.

I tried to push past. Sato stuck out his foot. I stumbled.

"Some stupid dancer!" Sato hooted. "Too stupid for any school."

I whipped around. "Leave me alone!"

He hit me square in the face. My mouth filled with blood. White pain shot through my jaw, filled my head.

I raised my arm, my warrior stick. Raised it high, ready to strike.

Someone grabbed me from behind and clasped my wrist.

My father. He pulled me back, stepped between me and Sato, bowing. My father, bowing! I wanted to spit. His hand gripped my wrist.

Sato swaggered closer, leering. "Look who's hiding behind his father like a scared little puppy."

A sharp whistle pierced the air. The crowd parted as Todaka-san strode toward us. Two soldiers approached my father. Both had rifles.

A tall figure pushed through the crowd, approached, bowed deeply. "I am very sorry, so very sorry. Please accept my apologies for my students' shameful behavior." Sensei spoke in the most respectful, most formal Japanese, stepping between my father and the marshal.

"Please forgive and understand. These are my students, and yes, this young dancer means no harm. Foolish boys full of sake, here to celebrate the Emperor's great and powerful army. To mar the beauty of this event is unnecessary. Here stands the chief of this village, leader of the dancers, a man who also celebrates the peaceful coexistence of the great people of Japan and the workers of this island." More bows, more pompous words of honor I could never utter.

Sensei motioned to my father, who bowed low and long, his head nearly touching his knees. Slowly my father moved backwards, pulling me with him. He did not stop retreating, head down, until we were far from the crowd. Finally he released my arm, stood tall and straight, and walked toward the sea. I followed. Once we were far from the village at an isolated area of beach, he stopped.

"Joseph ... Joseph," he said, his head shaking, his

voice discouraged, "your actions are selfish. Dangerous. Only a fool strikes without thinking."

"I didn't—"

"You raised your warrior stick as if to strike. For that action, you could have lost your life, and ours." My father looked exhausted. "Courage sometimes means to wait, even hide. A warrior listens to the dance within, not the buzzing around his ears. Joseph, give me your dancing stick."

I held it out.

"This dancing stick is a warrior's spear, his weapon to protect his clan and family." My father took my dancing stick, raised it high over his head, and struck it full force against the trunk of a tree. The stick shattered.

"Joseph, do you see these pieces? Broken. Worthless. To be a true warrior you must consider all consequences of your actions. Your anger can blind you."

He put his hands on my shoulders and spoke slowly, his words now gentle. "You are young, eager for adventure, ready to be trained for your first ocean voyage. But there is no time." He stared at the leaping surf, the resilient sea. "War is coming, Joseph. There are many soldiers, many ships, many planes. Be cautious, my son. Do not trust anyone who is not family. Even Kento and his sister. War turns everyone into soldiers, even children."

We stood in silence—silence as frightening and dark as the deep ocean.

"I must join the other men at the *Uut*. Go home and watch over our family. Make certain that Anna Maria is safe. The soldiers are full of sake."

I had been blind, like a turtle that stares into the sun.

My father left. I stayed, not ready to leave. In the distance, dogs barked. Roosters crowed, cockfighting fowls screeching challenges to each other: *fight me!* In the fighting ring, face to face, they did not cower. Did not hide. They fought until one lay dead.

I heard footsteps. Not soundless steps like my father's, but leather-soled boots that slapped against the wet sand. I wore shoes like those to school. I had tucked them high in the rafters of our hut. I would not wear them again until school reopened. Somehow I would learn without shoes. I would learn and become as powerful as those who had made us into their servants.

Kento approached, bowed.

I stared as if we were strangers, as if I had never really seen him before. How different we looked. No one would guess we were cousins; our mothers, sisters. He wore a clean-pressed shirt. My chest was bare and glistened with sweat and coconut oil. My hands were rough, coconut brown, and calloused from carrying breadfruit, wood for building huts and canoes. His hands were pale and smooth, stained with ink from writing kanji. We stood eye to eye, the same height, black eyes, black hair. His hair was straight, short and combed; mine was wild, still crowned with a flowered wreath from the dance. How different our worlds had become.

"Joseph, I am sorry."

I raised my eyebrows, acknowledging his words.

"I was afraid for you."

"No one needs to be afraid for me. No one!"

"I am glad you and your father did not get arrested."

I kicked at the sand. The sun was already low. Its light, reflected off the waves, glared in my eyes.

"Joseph, remember our secret cove?"

"We were silly kids."

"We had big plans, big dreams. Remember?"

I smiled. "You were going to be an engineer, like your father, and build some kind of crazy airplane."

Kento grinned back. "Crazy enough to fly to the moon."

Again, a slight raise of my eyebrows, my jaw set, but inside, such longing.

"You wanted to go to a big university, become a professor, start a school here."

I scooped up fistfuls of sand and threw them at the waves. "Now I can't even go to school."

"This difficult time can't last, Joseph." Kento stepped closer. "I don't want to lose my friend."

I looked at Kento and nodded. "You are brave ... like a samurai ... to come here and risk being seen with me." My voice was half angry, half sad. Was Kento here as a friend or as a spy?

The low light of dusk danced on the waves. So many times as children we had spent long afternoons at this beach, playing games, even games of war.

Kento spoke again, almost whispering. "Joseph, I need your help."

"Help from me, a stupid native?"

"In the canoe, you taught me about being a warrior. Teach me more. Teach me how to find food, to survive here on land."

"Your father is Japanese, part of the military. Go to one of your fancy stores for food."

"*All* stores are closed now, even ours."

I stared at Kento. Was he telling the truth?

"Joseph, your family needs rice and information. I need to learn to fish and find fresh water. To find coconuts and breadfruit."

Waves crashed, splashed high, rolled in, slipped out. Kento was right. Our family did need rice ... and information.

"Joseph, listen to me. My father makes reports for headquarters—how many soldiers, how many guns, how many more ships arrive. Preparations for battle, Joseph. War is coming. Here. Soon."

So it was true that Kento's father was a spy. Stay away, my father warned, a spy is dangerous to both friend and enemy. "You want something. What is it?"

Kento spoke softly. "My family needs your help. I come as a friend."

I turned away and stared at the sea as the last of the day's golden light danced on the waves.

"Joseph, every day when my father leaves, we know he might not return. Teach me so I can protect my family. I will pay with rice, tea, cooking oil." Kento looked at me, his eyes pleading.

"Pay me?"

"Yes, every day, rice, two large handfuls. Good rice. No stones or bugs. And when we can, oil and tea." Kento bowed. "My family needs fish, taro, anything fresh. Joseph, I ask you, as does my mother. She sends blessings to your family, to your sister, and promises to send plenty of rice."

I had no choice. If his mother, a sister to my mother, a member of our clan, asked, I must help.

"Teach me to write," I challenged him. "And I will teach you how to survive."

"You? Learn kanji! To read and write in Japanese? It isn't allowed. If we are caught—"

"We will meet at the cove, at night. If someone asks, we are searching for the tide pool shells so delicious to eat."

Kento hesitated. Finally he spoke. "When shall we begin?"

"Tonight, Kento, after curfew."

姐 SISTER

Black butterflies,
Typhoon winds tear
Silken wings,
Tomorrow
Upon red blossoms
You will dance.

I walked back to the village, looking for my father. He was not home but was still with the other men, Ignacio, too, gathered at the *Uut*, talking, arguing, all in hushed voices. For the first time, I wanted to slip in, sit with them, and listen. But I was not yet a warrior, not yet one of them.

My mother and Taeyo were already sleeping. But Anna Maria was missing. Father had instructed, *make sure your sister is safe.* She should be home.

I wandered the edges of our village. The air stilled. The day cooled. The sun paused on the horizon's rim, blazed gold, then slipped out of sight. Night would come quickly; already the half moon shone high above. Soon it would be curfew, time for everyone, especially women, to be home ... time to meet Kento at the cove.

I walked along the beach that curved away from our village toward the south. Someone stood there alone. It was my sister, waiting as she did each evening for Ignacio to return from the cane fields.

My mysterious sister was so much like our mother, quiet and shy. When she spoke, her words did not have hard edges like Japanese words. Her words were round, soft, slow. I stood in silence next to a tall coconut and watched as she waded through the lapping waves, splashing her face and her arms.

During the day, Anna Maria worked with our mother, sitting cross-legged, in the shade of a tall breadfruit tree, scraping coconut, preparing fresh thatch or, most often, weaving. They wove with a steady rhythm, bent over their work, their foreheads nearly touching, their black hair twisted in thick knots. They talked, laughing and nodding. What thoughts did they share?

She had always cared about me. When I was little, she would search for me after I had received a harsh scolding. She would sit nearby and sing. She spoke to me—not with words, but with a glance, a slight smile, a raised eyebrow. When my pouting stopped, she would hand me a coconut shell filled with seawater to wash and cool my face.

Weeks ago when our village celebrated Palm Sunday, her eyes had sparkled happily. Anna Maria had braided fronds for each of us to carry. She wore a white lace veil over her long black hair that fell down her back, past her hips, and she had tucked a bright red hibiscus behind her ear. She walked tall and proud, her hair loose, swaying with each step. During the entire procession to the church, she smiled at Ignacio. I could feel their longing as their eyes seemed to speak to each other. Would someone smile like that at me someday? When Ignacio teased her about how she liked showing off her hair, how it gleamed as it swayed, she frowned. He laughed, pretending to chase her. I pretended not to notice.

A few days later, our church was closed. Mass was forbidden. Our priest and nuns were arrested. Ignacio was ordered to work in the cane fields. Each morning now he left before light. Every evening Anna Maria waited here for his return.

Someone tapped my shoulder. I spun around.

Wide, frightened eyes met mine.

"Ako! What are you doing here? Your brother was supposed to meet me, not you. Not here! It's too dangerous."

"Sh-sh-sh. We must whisper." Ako stepped closer. In the moonlight I could barely see her round face, her serious mouth. Her chin trembled. "Soldiers are everywhere." She pointed up the hill toward her home—square, cement, solid, and Japanese.

"Where's Kento?"

She shook her head, "Too many soldiers guard our house tonight because of the new orders."

"What new orders?"

She placed a parcel in my hand. "My mother sends rice. She says, 'Remind Joseph, in our clan, if someone has food, everyone eats.'"

"Ako, what orders?"

"More soldiers have arrived." She put her finger to her lips. "They watched me run to the beach. They think children know nothing about war." She stood taller, pulled back her shoulders. "Girls can be soldiers, too."

"Ako, you must go home. Now!"

She shook her head again. Her long braids whipped back and forth, each braid tied with a bright yellow ribbon. "Joseph, the cave is too dangerous."

"Cave? What cave? What are you talking about?"

"Your father goes there—to the cave. My mother and I see him when we gather healing herbs on the hillside every morning before dawn. Your father often hurries through the jungle with bundles of coconuts." Ako bowed. "Mother says many will run to the caves. Soldiers will shoot them. Please, Joseph, come to our house before bombs fall everywhere. Father has a safe place for us."

As soundlessly as she had appeared, she left. For a moment, I could see the reflection of moonlight on her yellow ribbons. Like pale butterflies, the ribbons danced … and then disappeared from sight.

After my sister washed, she left the beach and walked toward home. I watched to be sure that no one came near, waited, then I also returned home. Everyone was sleeping; Taeyo now slept curled up next to his mother. But still no sign of Father and Ignacio. What were the men discussing so long? Rumors of fighting were flying like sparks through our village. I collapsed on my sleeping mat, closed my eyes, but could not rest, questions kept spinning. What orders? Why more soldiers? And what cave?

旅 JOURNEY

Geckos chirped,
Kingfishers squawked,
Dogs barked.
This is home.
War cannot come here.
Cannot.

Someone was shaking me.

I woke with a start. It was still dark.

"Joseph, get up. Follow me."

I rolled over, confused.

"Hurry. We must leave." My father handed me a bowl of water. "We have a hard journey."

He waited as I gulped down the water and splashed the last of it on my face.

"You are a good son, Joseph. Today you must learn quickly."

I pulled on a shirt and shorts and followed him out the door. We hurried away from the village, following the shoreline and then zigzagging up the cliffs. He picked his way up the steep slope, bent over, head down, keeping close to the thick brush, staying concealed. I mimicked his every move, struggling to keep up, determined to show him I could, and all the time wondering, where are we going?

He kept climbing. He never glanced back to see if I followed. Even though I moved as silently as possible, he could hear me. We continued climbing away from our village, away from the sea. I hadn't gone this way since the Japanese forbade us to go where they were digging foxholes or building thick-walled cement bunkers. Why would my father risk being sighted here and shot?

We came to a shallow ravine. Soon the rainy season would turn this dry gully into a slick muddy wash. My father followed the ravine uphill, keeping his head lower than the grasses that lined each side. He signaled, frowning, never speaking: *Stay lower. Don't stop. Hurry.* We continued climbing up and up. A few times he paused, surveyed the area we had crossed, and then continued.

Within an hour we were halfway up this steep rugged side of the island, the western shoulder of Mount Tapotchau. Night's darkness changed to the colorless gray of predawn. The ravine ended, and two paths branched in opposite directions. One path veered north, a path I now recognized. Father and I had hiked that way on a journey across the island's entire length. That path wound upward through sugarcane fields until it reached the island's most northern point. There a flat grassy savanna led to cliffs that plunged straight down hundreds of feet.

At the edge of that cliff my father and I had stood side by side and stared down at that murderous drop to jagged rocks and a frothing ocean. I shivered, remembering Father's warning: "Don't ever come to these cliffs again, Joseph. Older boys sneak away to hunt here. Don't be tempted. This is a place of death. Listen to the wind, to White Woman's hungry scream." He pointed at several pairs of fairy terns swooping up and down the precipice's sheer face. "See, they call to the lost souls who forever search for home."

Below us huge swells swept in and burst into sprays of white as they crashed against black boulders. Pools of foam swirled, disappeared; another swell swept across the surface.

No, I never wanted to return to that terrible place.

The other trail joined the village path that led across the island's southern shoulder. One dry season Ignacio and I had taken it to the top of Mount Tapotchau. That was before Ignacio became my sister's husband, when he told me about *luus*, the game of finding someone to love, of how he had chased and captured my sister, and during the night that followed, they had talked and laughed, teased and chased some more and decided to marry. I blushed even now remembering.

My father didn't take either path. He headed straight up through the jungle. Thick vines looped and crisscrossed everywhere, growing over everything, suffocating trees, turning them into green headless monsters. We climbed over knife-sharp rock, pushed our way through thorny bushes. My feet burned. My arms and legs were covered with red welts. Even my chest hurt from wanting more breath. Where were we going?

Father stopped.

What? I signaled. He didn't answer; he stood and listened.

I smelled the water before I saw it. We pushed through a screen of vegetation. This is why we had stopped here. Water trickled from the rocks and pooled in a bed of green moss.

"Remember this place, Joseph. Thirst kills. Water is life. This is the only water near the cave." He searched my face. "Do you understand?"

What cave? What am I supposed to understand? But I didn't ask. I dipped my fingers in the pool and touched them to my lips.

"Drink, Joseph. Drink your fill."

He didn't need to ask again. I cupped my hands and gulped mouthful after mouthful.

My father drank, nodded to me, then pushed back the ferns and vines and continued up, even faster than before. At first my legs refused to move. Where were we going?

Father paused when we reached a narrow footpath that continued across the face of a crumbling limestone cliff. We stayed low, picked our way across, all the time staying hidden behind a veil of hanging vines. Past the cliff, the path opened into a small niche. Here we stopped. A hibiscus bush grew in one corner. Its red blossoms faced a beam of sunlight that broke through the curtain of green. Beautiful red flowers blooming in a place like this. What was wrong with me? I wanted to cry! Sweat covered my back, dripped down my face, and stung my eyes. Mosquitoes whined. Black flies buzzed and bit. I didn't care. I sat, staring at the delicate red blossoms. Then I realized the buzzing was not from flies. Overhead an airplane circled.

Down! Father signaled. We rolled under some vines, stayed facedown. Something touched my skin. A spider tiptoed up my arm. I closed my mind to everything but this spider and watched as its iridescent colors—green, blue, red—shimmered in the shifting splashes of sunlight. The spider scurried off a fingertip and was gone.

Silence. The plane was gone. My father sat up. His eyes searched every direction. Finally he spoke. "When the fighting begins, Joseph, hide our family in this cave."

I scrambled to my feet. *What was he talking about? Had Father lost his mind?* Behind me the cliff loomed straight up. Below us lay a jungle of green. There was no cave.

"Joseph, bring them here. Ignore what others say."

His words made no sense. Even if there was a cave, how could I ever bring them here—my mother who walked with back bent, and my sister heavy with the fullness of a child growing, and little Taeyo? My father and I had barely made it up the steep slope, pushing through walls of jungle.

How could I ever find this place? I shook my head, stared out over the steep green slope, wishing I could see the ocean, hear the surf, sounds and smells that meant home.

The sky had become a hot, bright blue. A fruit dove sang a morning song. Its mate answered. I saw their bright orange-red plumage as they chased between tree-tops. My father also stared toward an unseeable ocean as if trying to make a difficult decision. He turned toward me. His face softened as he spoke.

"Joseph, this cave has hidden our people during times of war. Bring our family here. Promise you will do this."

Many times my father had come home exhausted, but he'd never looked like this — resigned ... defeated. When had he become so old?

Salty winds from the sea swept up the hillside, cooling our faces, shaking the treetops. Bamboo clattered below us. My father's eyes searched each shadow.

"I may not be able to help you."

"But, Father—"

"No. Listen. We have little time." He pointed to the top of the cliff behind us. "The cave is up there. As soon as I am certain no one has followed us, we will climb to it."

"I don't understand—"

"Remember the turtle, Joseph. When the shark smells blood, he attacks. The turtle pulls in his head, waits ... survives. Joseph, survive. Bring our family here."

"But Kento's family can help us. They know where—"

"Don't trust anyone, Joseph! If Kento is forced to choose, will he choose our family or his? Taeyo or Ako? If the Japanese lose, they will destroy everyone just like they killed all the Koreans and Okinawans on Tinian. Even their own they will kill. Their code of honor demands this. Don't run to them for protection. Small fish that hide with the big ones are eaten."

"The Japanese are powerful. Kento says they cannot lose."

"Bring our family here, Joseph."

My father reached for the lowest limb of an old massive breadfruit tree, then scrambled from branch to branch until he disappeared into the leafy canopy. I followed. Halfway up the tree, cooler air rustled through the leaves. My father pushed aside a young branch; I stared at two flat slabs of stone that bordered a wide entrance. Rancid air hit my face. Several bats flew out. A black rat scrambled back into the shadows. I shuddered, then crawled in.

As my eyes adjusted to the dim light, I saw more. The cave was large, nearly the size of our hut. Piles of supplies were stacked along the walls: green coconuts, sugarcane, tinned meat, even bottles and gourds filled with water. How many trips had my father taken to bring all this here?

"Everything you will need is here. Food for one week

and water, if you ration carefully. A rock at the back covers a pit toilet. Keep it covered so the smell doesn't draw attention." My father nodded. "Sit down, Joseph, listen carefully." He reached behind one of the stacks of cane and slipped out his prize machete. "Now this is yours. A true warrior protects. I give it to you to safeguard our family, to find food. Tonight I must leave."

"Leave? Tonight? What are you talking about? We need you. We—"

"Imperial orders, delivered last night during the celebration. All adult men must go to the airfield to clear rocks for the new runways."

Everything started spinning. Leave? My father leave? To carry buckets of rock at the airfield in the hot sun? Cutting cane in the fields was killing Ignacio, and he was much younger than my father.

"I will go in your place."

My father placed his hands on my shoulders. "Such young shoulders for this difficult task." He breathed deeply, "My warrior son, protect our family. Use your head. Trees that bend survive the typhoon; those that resist, shatter."

"Please don't leave. Hide here."

He handed me a thick stalk of sugarcane. "Chew slowly. The sweetness soothes. If I am not with the other men, the soldiers will search our village, find that I am missing, and then punish our family. When the bombs begin to fall, bring our family here. This place has been our family's refuge for generations of ancestors. Wars have washed over our island like typhoons. Spanish, Germans, the Japanese, soon the Americans. Soldiers come, fight their battles, then leave. We are the ones who remain, if we hide and wait."

"Father—"

"My son, the Americans will invade. Our people mean nothing to either side, minnows caught in a cross-fire." He paused. "Survive, Joseph. See this cave in your mind. See it, and it will lead you here.

"War is coming. Both armies will fight until many have died, American and Japanese. Who will win the battles? I do not know. The Japanese are proud. Their obedience to their Emperor is total. They will be ordered to sacrifice everything for victory. Or everything because of defeat. Their lives, their people. Even their children. Joseph, even us. No place will be safe, Joseph."

"What about you and Ignacio?"

"When the rains begin, we will escape and look for you here." He turned his machete around so the handle faced me. "Leave this here. When you go out to hunt, blacken the blade so it does not reflect anything, not even the moonlight. Use it as a true warrior—to protect, never in haste."

"I don't know. ..."

"Sometimes you won't know." My father did not hurry his words. He spoke as if the two of us were in our canoe, paddling out to sea with a whole day to sail and look for turtle. "Listen, Joseph. Listen from within."

We left the cave. At the base of the tree, my father studied the ground looking for signs of anyone who may have followed us. He whispered, "Return to the ravine and follow it home. I will make a false trail. Go now."

"Disobey those orders, Father. Hide here."

"I cannot, Joseph. Our people have survived many generations. We watch, wait out the storm and do not fight the current's flow. Hide, Joseph, and survive." My father looked at me with eyes so tender I wanted to weep. "Joseph, remember the dance, and you will be able to fly. Remember the sea, and you will again dream. Remember the turtle, Joseph, and you will know how to wait."

He turned to the north, slipped through the bushes, and was gone.

I scrambled down the hillside, pushed through walls of foliage. Sweat stung the angry cuts that crisscrossed my arms.

How could I ever find my way back? I tried to pay attention to everything. That rock where I turned—how was it different from the others? Which tree signaled to veer south rather than continue straight down?

A distant droning grew louder. High above, planes flew in close formation, slips of silver like fairy terns. But these silver birds were not a welcome omen.

I pushed through more jungle, tripped and fell, digging my fingers into the rocky soil.

See this cave in your mind, see it.

A kingfisher squawked. How could war come here? The buzz of planes continued. I stared past the jungle, at the unseen ocean and the rows of waiting warships. And beyond them? Would American ships come here? How could my father leave us?

I stood back up and stared at the steep slope.

The cave was up there, but where?

We could survive in that cave.

I heard my father's words.

See it in your mind.

舞 DANCE!

Think only of the dance
That gives strength
To leap
To fly.

"Joseph!"

My eyes opened. I was home. Smoke swirled above me, the delicious sweet smoke from cooking fires.

"He's awake! Finally." Taeyo ducked through the door, leaped on top of me, and began pummeling me with his fists.

"Get up, Uncle Joe. Come outside. We're going to have a feast! Piles and piles of food. Crispy fat fish, sweet coconut pudding." Taeyo grinned, rubbing his tummy. "A feast for everyone!"

I sat up. "What are you talking about, Taeyo?"

He grabbed my hand and pulled me outside. "Before they leave. First we feast. Then we dance." Taeyo looked at me. "Why such a big frown, Uncle Joe? They'll come back soon. My mother said so."

My eyes squinted to keep out the bright glare. The sun was high overhead. How long had I been sleeping? I hurt all over; my arms were streaked with cuts and scratches. And then I remembered. The long climb to the cave ... the piles of food inside ... the scramble back down alone. Alone. Father was leaving tonight. Leaving.

Taeyo pulled me by my hand. "Look, Uncle Joe. Food everywhere!"

Stacks of food were piled near every door—green coconuts, dried fish, packets of salt. Green bananas hung from the door beams. Why so much food? Then I realized: food for the men to take with them.

"What's wrong, Uncle Joe? You are still frowning."

I looked down at Taeyo, rumpled his wild hair, and then stared at our village.

Cooking fires flickered near each home. Men stood in clusters, talking, stirring the coals, adding more coconut husks. The younger boys carried bunches of green coconuts on long sticks balanced across their shoulders. Dogs trotted after the children, sniffing for food, growling at each other until they were chased away with a stone or a shout. Pigs squealed. Chickens squawked.

The sharp smell of fried fish nearly made me faint. My stomach was so empty. The village was like a stirred-up anthill. Soldiers marched on every street, rifles over their shoulders. Wherever they walked, people parted around them like water before a ship.

My mother sat in the shade of a coconut palm, cleaning Father's ceremonial mat. Usually this special mat was kept rolled up, tied, and stored on top of a ceiling beam next to other important belongings: a basket of fine, nearly invisible fishing twine and hand-carved lures, sacred baskets that held bones of our ancestors, Father's long smooth dancing stick, and, usually, his machete.

Taeyo tugged at my shirt.

"Okay, okay, I'm coming. Be patient. I need to wash and wake up."

"What a sleepyhead for an uncle!" Taeyo laughed and ran off to beg bites of food from his favorite aunties or anyone else who couldn't resist his bright smile.

I wandered around in a daze. Everywhere women were busy, grinding coconut meat, squeezing coconut cream to add to bubbling pots of fish or green banana, pounding roasted breadfruit, rolling balls of boiled rice inside banana leaves. The delicious smells should have meant celebration, but nothing felt festive. People were quiet and especially gentle with one another.

My mother called to Anna Maria. "Go to the beach." She nodded toward Ignacio. "Take your husband. Find more octopus."

I understood. Anna Maria looked away, but I could see the glow on her face as she stood up. She followed close behind Ignacio as he walked with long, even strides. She had untied her hair.

My mother turned to me. "Good. You are awake." She didn't even scold. "We need pandanus leaves and hibiscus for the dancers, for their head wreaths, the *mwaars*. But first gather more coconuts. Today, the

soldiers said, no rules, no curfews. We can go anywhere."
My mother smiled. "Take Taeyo."

"Taeyo?"

"Take him. He is pestering everyone."

"I need a machete. ..." I glanced at my father.

"Ignacio gave permission to use his. And today it is allowed." My father nodded.

"Come on, Taeyo. Let's go. First coconuts and then pandanus."

Taeyo bounced beside me like a puppy. Excited, happy, not understanding. He was still a child. We walked past family after family busily preparing for the evening, and I felt as if stones filled my chest.

We headed straight into the thick bush behind the village where the ground was black and marshy, where a small grove of coconut palms grew hidden between thickets of bamboo. Several young ylang-ylang trees also grew here, and their blossoms sweetened the air. A fruit dove sang out, and for a moment I could again see the cave and hear my father's words: *Hide until the storm passes. Remember the turtle; become the turtle.* Would our family be safe in such a place?

"What's wrong, Uncle Joe?" Taeyo asked. "Why are we standing here?"

"Just thinking. Here, want to carry the machete?"

"Really?"

"Be careful. It's your father's. Keep the sharp edge

pointed down. Don't drop it on your toes. Remember, it is an honor to carry someone's machete."

Taeyo grinned, stood straighter. He walked by my side, his head held high like mine, stretching his legs to match mine, and for a few wonderful quiet minutes he did not say a word.

"There. See those two young trees hidden among the bamboo? I've been keeping an eye on them. They're heavy with ripe nuts. Perfect for today."

"Good eyes, Uncle Joe! They're hard to see."

"Good eyes, yourself! Okay, let's see how strong you are. Climb up, and I'll hand you the machete. Just don't drop it on my head. Cut enough coconuts for today. Then toss them to me. The rest we'll save for some other time."

Taeyo slipped through the bamboo like a skinny lizard, then shinnied to the top of the first palm. "Watch out—here they come!" He threw down one heavy nut after another, aiming for my head, laughing each time I ducked. How long had it been since I had felt silly-happy like that?

"Enough! Enough! Come back down. We have plenty to carry."

Taeyo wiggled down, leaped the last few feet to the ground, and stood straight, chest out, and grinned even wider.

"Good work. Give me back that machete. We'll cut two bamboo stalks, tie on the coconuts, and you can carry them home!" I teased and then thought of the dozens of coconuts my father had stacked in the cave. For an instant I saw them, saw the cave, the rat escaping out the entrance. The machete fell from my hand, barely missing my foot.

"What's wrong, Uncle Joe?"

"Nothing, Taeyo, nothing. We forgot to give thanks to the spirits for all this food." Taeyo solemnly bowed his head and crossed himself as if in church. How strange to be the older one, the teacher.

I stooped over to pick up the machete. *Thunk!*

I looked up and heard it again. *Thunk!* Then the bamboo stalks began clattering. Someone was moving through the thicket. Soldiers weren't supposed to bother us today, but ... I glanced at Taeyo and raised my eyebrows: don't move. *Thunk!* Something was being whacked. Hard.

"Who's there? Show yourself!" I pushed Taeyo behind me.

Clackety, click, click, click. Bamboo knocked and rattled.

"Speak!" I ordered with the machete held high.

The bamboo separated; a face peered out.

Taeyo laughed. I breathed out and lowered the machete.

Two dark braids tied with yellow ribbons framed Ako's face. Her eyes sparkled with mischief.

"Ako-chan! What are you doing here?"

Ako slipped out between the last few stalks. She held up a large coconut crab with a cracked shell.

"You're too little to be out here alone. Where's Kento?"

Ako grinned even broader. "Kento is afraid a coconut crab will pinch his toes. And I am *not* little! Most every morning when it's still dark I come here with Mama-oma to find the healing plants. The medicine inside them is stronger before the sun heats them. Sometimes I come here by myself when soldiers order Oma to stay at the house."

I shook my head. "It's too dangerous here, what if—"

"I'm not afraid. Not like Kento, even though he's older. Anyway, it is better to be little. I can slip into places where coconut crabs hide." She held her prize catch over her head. The crab's legs dangled down past her nose.

"You caught that big crab yourself? Those big ones are mean!"

"And delicious."

Taeyo reached to touch a wiggling leg.

"No!" Ako cried. "That claw could snap off your finger." She frowned at Taeyo, then held the crab so he could take a close look. "Isn't it beautiful? Yesterday I left bait here. Coconut meat. Today—*whack!* A few hits with a rock and ... supper!" She grinned. "Why are you here?"

I pointed to the stack of coconuts.

"For tonight?" Her voice was suddenly serious and sad.

"Yes, for tonight." I didn't want to talk about it.

"Okay, Taeyo, our mothers are waiting. Quick, pick some flowers for the wreaths. There's some hibiscus—choose only the biggest blossoms, only the red ones—and I'll get the ylang-ylang."

"What about her?" Taeyo frowned at Ako.

I looked at Ako. "Walk back with us. Taeyo can carry that crab for you."

"I can carry it myself."

Taeyo gave me a disgusted look. I raised my eyebrows. He didn't say anything but snatched blossom after blossom, frowning the whole time.

"Ako, where is Kento?"

"Pounding rice into *mochi*. Father came home early this morning, but he has to leave already tonight. Kento is making *mochi* for father to take with him. Mother and I are cooking this crab." Ako paused, then spoke very seriously. "My family thanks you again. You saved Kento from the sea."

"How do you know about that? Kento was not to tell anyone."

Ako looked surprised and stared at me. Strange how sometimes she looked so much older, her face serious like an adult.

"Joseph, are you blind? Don't you see there are no secrets? Not on this island."

"Uncle Joe, did you really save Kento from the sea? When, Uncle Joe?"

"Never mind, Taeyo."

My little nephew scowled like an old man. "Nobody ever answers my questions anymore!"

Ako stared at me. "Think about what my mother said. The caves are not safe." She nodded. "Come with us." Ako bowed then slipped through the thick bamboo and was gone.

"What caves, Uncle Joe?"

"I have no idea," I lied.

"I'm hungry, Uncle Joe."

"You'll fill your stomach soon enough. Let's gather up everything and head home." Home ... my father would not be at home after tonight. I pushed that thought as far away as possible. Still, I felt as if someone had punched me hard in the stomach.

Our arms full, we started back. Taeyo barely kept up; he was tired. We bundled up his load, and he held it on his head, but with each step, flowers or leaves slipped down, leaving a trail behind us. He'd stop to pick them up. Then more would fall. "Taeyo, keep walking or we will never get home!"

Already the sun sat low in the sky, a hazy ball of fire pouring across the water and transforming the waves into glowing embers. This was the time of day Father and I should be wading out to fish the reef. He would laugh each time the surf lifted us up and dropped us back down, and then he would tease because my eyes kept watching for a dark fin slicing across the surface. How childish my old fears seemed.

"Taeyo, we dance as warriors tonight. I need to prepare my mind, my spirit, all of me, for the dance. You go on ahead home. I need to be alone."

Taeyo frowned again but started toward the village.

I turned and faced the sea.

The tide was coming in. The surf rolled over the reef, curled higher, the inside dark blue, the crest thin and white. Then *crash!*—the surf crackled, froth spilled, tumbled, and then slipped back. I longed to make this day stop, make time pause, let the endless singing of the surf soothe my fears, but nothing stopped the sun ... nothing stopped the sea.

"Joseph, my son."

I spun around. My father stood before me, tall and proud. Lines of red paint streaked down each cheek; pandanus leaves hung from his arms, wrists, and thighs. His dark skin glistened with oil.

"You are preparing yourself for the dance. Good. Sit with me. Tonight I will tell you the story of our ancestors one more time."

He began as he had so many times before. But tonight it felt different.

"It came in a dream," my father said. "It came in a dream to one of our long-ago ancestors. Clansmen had been warring. Too many had died from the fighting, from the starvation that followed. Too many people, gone."

My father lowered his voice, hesitated, then continued. "A stranger came, and this spirit commanded,

'Get up! In the darkness of the night, get up!'"

My father paused, swallowed hard, stared at the horizon.

"Yes, I remember, Father." I picked up the familiar string of words. "And then the spirit began to dance, chanting and inviting—'Dance with me. Leap and strike your warrior spears. Faster, faster, yes! Strike harder, leap higher!'" Now I paused, trying to remember the chants, the rhythm of the stamping and slapping, the striking of the sticks.

My father nodded for me to continue.

"All through the night they danced, and then again the spirit spoke. 'Teach your people. Learn these dances. Protect your clan. This is your hope for survival. Light the fire within you. Light the bonfire that we might see. Learn to sweep, to leap, to fly—'"

My father placed both hands on my shoulders. "Yes, Joseph, tonight we will light the bonfires that we might see. I will blow the great conch shell. Our people will gather. We will leap and shout, hit against each other's warrior spears, call to our ancestors, dancing faster, whirling, leaping higher until our lungs burn ... our bodies shine with sweat. But we will not fight. We will put down our warrior spears, our weapons. This is our hope for survival. We will hold our heads high as we walk into the night, into the darkness.

"Joseph, our ancestors' dance happened hundreds of years ago." He waited, watched my face. "Still they dance." My father asked, "Did it happen at all?"

I stared at my feet, dug my toes into the cool wet sand, but did not answer.

"Keep the words within you, Joseph. When you are lost in darkness that you do not understand, listen for them. Do you understand?"

I still could not answer.

He nodded to the sea, to the waves that washed over our feet. "You will hear them and you will know."

勇 勇気 COURAGE

Old turtle,
Little crab,
Where should I go?
Where can I hide?

One week passed. No word about anyone: not my father, not Ignacio. Nothing.

The buzz of airplanes became part of our world. Planes streaked low and spat out fire, stinking the air with black fumes. Ships—steel sharks—appeared along the horizon and waited. In our village there was no food. There were more soldiers. To the south, explosions sent orange smoke toward us. We could smell war.

Suddenly, the soldiers left. We could think of no good reason for this. Their absence felt stranger than their presence. Soon new soldiers patrolled the beach but only at night during curfew. These replacements were strangers and marched with straight backs, eyes narrowed as they scanned the shoreline. Were they looking for enemy soldiers or spies from our village? Their hands gripped rifles. They did not speak, but they were no older than my classmates.

Each day I became bolder. We needed food. I took

Taeyo with me to secret places to show him where to dig taro. I told him, "Remember this place."

"Why, Uncle Joe?"

"Remember it, Taeyo. See it in your mind so you can find it."

The women gathered, anxiously talked more openly—in front of the closed church, the boarded-up stores, even in the middle of the road in front of the patrols. Who had news of the men? Was it true that the Japanese had guns longer than coconut trees? Had the other islanders, the Chamorros, even the priests and holy sisters been taken as prisoners ... or put to death! Could that be? Someone had seen many planes marked with the round red sun of Japan, flying low, burning, falling from the sky. Was that possible? The women chewed every splinter of news like starving dogs gnawing on bones.

Then news came from a surprise visitor. I had wandered far from the village toward town to gather healing leaves from a special vine. "In case we need medicine for wounds," my mother had instructed. I had followed the shoreline and began to feel uneasy. Someone was following me, someone who didn't want to be seen.

I left the open beach and took a shortcut back home, a path that led through heavy foliage.

"Joseph."

I turned.

"Don't be alarmed. I am here as a friend."

"Sensei!"

"I didn't mean to frighten you. I waited until we would not be noticed."

I had forgotten my manners and quickly bowed. "I ... I hope you are well."

"Listen carefully, Joseph. I must return to Garapan before my absence is noticed."

"But—"

"No, just listen. Last week a major air battle was fought and lost. Soon many American planes will begin bombing."

"Bombing? I don't understand."

"Bombing this island. Saipan is strategic to the American military, one island closer to their invasion of Japan." Sensei's eyes never stopped glancing and searching.

"Please, Joseph, tell no one you saw me here. Do you understand?"

"I understand." The rumors were true. Burning planes had fallen from the sky.

"After bombing the beaches, the Americans will invade. Go somewhere away from the sea, far from the shore. The first battles will be fought along the shoreline. Don't get caught in the crossfire."

I thought of the cave. Was it far enough from the sea?

Sensei looked down, then cleared his throat. "Yesterday I saw your father and Ignacio at the airstrip. I could not speak to them—"

"They are alive! Do they know about the bombs, the invasion?"

He did not answer. Sensei shook his head and handed me a small package. "For you, Joseph. Always remember what a fine student you are. I have marked my favorite poem, 'An ancient pond. A frog jumps in. The splash of water.' That is your challenge, the splash of water." Sensei bowed. "Now I must go. I have my duty, I must obey."

When I returned home, I feared it all had been a dream. But hidden under my sleeping mat, my fingers touched the small book and told me the truth. Bashö's book of poems was safe.

The days were long, the nights, longer. Often I awoke from the same nightmare. I watched my father walk away. *Come back*, but he would not stop. He was swallowed by dark, swirling surf. I tried to reach out, to pull him back; I could not move.

As soon as each day ended and the firewood was stacked, taro dug, and coconuts gathered, I slipped down to the cove to meet Kento. It felt good to break curfew, to defy one rule. No one bothered us except Taeyo and Ako. No matter how much we threatened, they showed up. Ako slipped through the night like a shadow. Taeyo rattled every branch and vine. They mostly kept quiet as they practiced skipping stones and writing kanji in the sand.

Every evening Kento taught me letters, and I taught him to crack a coconut without losing a drop of juice, to dig taro without bruising the root, and where to find the hidden springs of fresh water.

"Remember, Kento, coconut meat is food. The milk inside is water rich with energy. If you have a breadfruit tree and three coconut palms, you can survive anything."

I showed him the little shells that cling to the undersides of sea rocks and how to find an octopus hidden in dark crevices of coral. He was afraid to grab the soft head and bite off the sharp beak. He learned.

"Kento, tell me about the battles, the ships. Are they coming closer?" He would not say.

"Joseph, if there are battles, they will begin in the south."

"In the south, near the airfields? Why?"

"That is the best place to invade. The beaches there are wide and shallow, easier for the Americans to unload their soldiers and quickly attack. But it is very exposed." Kento looked away, mumbled, "Easier for us to gun them down."

"Us?"

"Will they shoot at us?" Taeyo piped in.

Kento turned away.

The rains began and fell steadily. Still no message from Father or Ignacio ... *when the season of the rain begins, we will escape* ... they must still be alive, they must. Sensei had seen them. Rain splashed on the roof and ran in rivulets around our home. Water would now be rushing down that ravine and the steep path to the cave would be slippery with mud. How could my family climb up that muck? How would I find the cave?

One evening Kento came alone.

"Where is Ako?"

"Home. Tonight Mother forbade her to come."

Taeyo tugged at my shirt. "Shall I get her?"

"No! Not tonight. Too many soldiers." Kento turned to me. "Tonight let me teach you how to be a samurai, a true warrior."

"I am a true warrior."

"Yes, but listen. You, too, Taeyo. Long ago in Japan, the great warriors, the samurai, learned many kinds of battle skills. They learned to focus completely on the smallest details—to focus until their thinking was as sharp as any sword ... or as hot as fire."

"We do the same when we prepare to dance: light the fire within you, touch your spirit ... fly ... words my father said that at first made no sense."

"My father said, 'If you can focus, you can endure.'" Kento pointed to a little hole in the sand by my foot, the home of a ghost crab. "Watch. When the crab comes out, study every detail: how it moves, where it hides. Think only about that one tiny creature. Become that creature."

"Become a ghost crab? Why?"

"Let nothing else come into your thoughts. Focus. Then imagine words. Write them. When you write, my father says you discover truths, something known but unknown to you." Kento wrote several columns of kanji. "Like this, a poem for us."

> *Ghost crabs*
> *Racing bowlegged, sideways, tiptoed,*
> *Pop*
> *Into holes,*
> *Survive.*

"Like this, Uncle Joe!" Taeyo began racing across the beach, sideways on all fours like a giant crab.

"Taeyo, stop! Be still. Be quiet." I frowned at Kento. "So, we must become crabs ... or ghosts?"

Before he could answer, we heard the sound of booted footsteps crackling through the brush.

"Halt. Stand straight," a soldier snapped. "It is past curfew."

A second soldier stepped out of the shadows. "Children! Foolish children. This place is off-limits, forbidden. Go home. Go now!"

My hands fisted, but I kept my mouth shut.

"Go home!" He pointed toward the village.

We began to walk away. "Don't talk, stay next to me," I ordered Taeyo.

Someone was running down the beach in clear view of everyone. We stopped. The soldiers shifted their rifles. I held Taeyo's arm.

"Kento! Joseph!" Ako shouted between gulps of air. "We must leave! We must leave!" Then Ako saw the soldiers. She also stopped, stood still.

I turned to Taeyo. "Go home before there is trouble. Kento and I will take Ako home. We need to talk. Tell Anna Maria I will be home soon."

"But—"

"Go." I pointed.

Taeyo frowned. Then he slipped through the trees and soon was out of sight.

Kento and I hurried back down the beach with Ako between us. When we were out of sight of the soldiers, I whispered, "Ako, what happened?"

She struggled to get the words out, shaking her head, brushing away tears. "Soldiers. At our house."

"What do you mean?"

"They said, 'Pack—prepare to leave.'"

"Leave?" I glanced from Ako to Kento.

"Are they going to arrest us, Kento, or shoot us?"

"Hush." Kento warned. "Father has a safe place for us. Joseph, you and your family join us. The caves are not safe."

Ako blurted out, "Remember what I told you, what Mother said."

A gunshot exploded nearby.

A child screamed.

I could not move, could not breathe. A child cried, and I knew that cry.

"Taeyo!"

FATHER

Night gives way to day,
And death
To life.

I carried Taeyo home. As soon as he had his arms around
my neck, he clung so tight I could hardly breathe. I softly
chanted a warrior song, and soon he stopped crying.
My sister met us not far from our hut. Once inside, she
rolled out a mat, and I set Taeyo down. Blood oozed from
his leg. Anna Maria brought water, soap, strips of cloth,
and vine leaves, healing herbs, pounded into a poultice.
The bullet had gone through the side of his leg below his
knee, not deep. A clean wound. After she washed his leg,
treated it with the herbs, and bandaged it, the bleeding
barely oozed. Taeyo slept. Anna Maria sat by his side,
massaging his arms with one hand, holding the round-
ness of her belly with the other.

My mother brought water. "Drink, Joseph."

"I shouldn't have sent him home alone."

"Joseph, we do not know what is on the other side of
a decision." She urged me to drink more water. "No one
can change from boy to man in a single day."

I sat with my arms wrapped around my head. My world had become crazy. How could anyone shoot a child? What did Ako mean that they had to leave? Should we go with them? But would they protect us? How could I ever find the cave? What did Sensei say? But what if the Japanese lost? No, that could never happen. I tried to think. I wanted to cry. Where would our family be safe?

I did not mean to sleep.

I woke up coughing, choking on smoke. Was this another nightmare? Smoke burned my throat and eyes. The earth trembled. The screams were real. I ran outside.

Flares shot across the early morning sky, but it was not a sky I recognized. The southern horizon glowed orange, as if it were burning. An orange that was wrong, that smelled like death. The south ... the airfield ... my father ... Ignacio. Another explosion shook the earth. Black smoke poured across the southern horizon. Tongues of flames shot up, disappeared, reappeared.

My mother and sister were outside. They stood holding each other, staring south. I looked toward the reef. Giant ships, steel gray, crowded along the reef—so many, so huge. Streams of fire and smoke exploded from them, above them. Where had they come from? Were these American? Why hadn't the Japanese stopped them? People were running out from their homes, babies were crying, children screaming. *What should I do?* Ako had urged, "Come with us." But I promised Father I would go to the cave.

People trudged past, carrying children. So many faces streaked with soot and tears. Some saw me and shouted, "We are leaving! We are leaving! Come with us."

I looked at my mother. She shook her head.

Women ran past carrying mats, bundles of food. One walked beside a wooden cart pulled by a water buffalo. A black dog trotted behind, its belly swollen, soon to have puppies. How would they survive? I turned to my mother. "We must leave."

"Soon." She continued to roll up another mat, wrap another packet of baked breadfruit in banana leaves. "Taeyo is resting. His wound will soon stop bleeding."

"We will wait a few hours," I said. "No more. After the moon rises, we will leave. Even with the rain, the moonlight will help us find the way." *How will I ever find the way?*

Explosions continued. Ugly curls of smoke smeared the southern sky. Ashes fell with the rain. We stayed busy with preparations for leaving. We did not speak. Taeyo barely stirred. Outside, people were walking, running, and carrying bundles on their backs or little children on their shoulders.

Roosters crowed, dogs barked. The familiar sounds made me shiver. How many days since my father and Ignacio had left? Maybe twenty, maybe more. Every evening my sister had cut a mark on the breadfruit tree outside our house. Even now she went outside and made one more mark, then continued on to the shore.

"Don't let her go there," I urged my mother. "It is too dangerous."

"Let her be." My mother followed and stood near my sister. I stared at their silhouettes. I went back inside and checked on Taeyo. Good, he was sleeping. I slipped my hand under my sleeping mat and my fingers found the familiar shape, Sensei's book. I held it for a moment, then tucked it in with our things. I heard a noise and looked up.

Someone stepped into our hut and stood before me, dripping with rain. An old man, a skeleton covered with skin.

My father had come home.

He stepped toward me and collapsed. I caught him and held his shivering body against mine as if he were a child. I tried to say his name, but nothing came out. He lifted his arm, pressed his hand on my lips, and whispered, "Joseph. Listen ... listen."

His voice was barely more than a rattle.

Word by word, he struggled to speak. "Tell Anna Maria. Joseph, tell her."

"Tell her what, Father?"

"Soldiers saw us. Running." He closed his eyes and breathed several times before he could speak again. "Soldiers beat us, left us to die. I did not die. Tell Anna Maria."

My father pulled my face close to his. He spoke

slowly. "Darkness came. I woke up. Ignacio was gone. I called. Then I heard them, Joseph, the chants. They led me home."

My father stopped. His gaze shifted. He stared at something behind me.

My mother screamed. She ran to my father, sat beside him, cradled his head.

"Water!" my mother cried. My father needed water.

Anna Maria handed me a gourd filled with fresh water. I had not heard my sister re-enter the room. She stood behind me, her head bowed. Her hands were trembling. She looked at me, questioning.

"Ignacio?" she whispered.

I looked away and held the gourd to my father's lips. He swallowed like a child, water spilling down his chin. This broken man was my father. It could not be.

My sister waited. I did not know what to say.

My mother bathed him. She massaged his bruised skin, first with water from the sea and then with coconut oil, her fingers rubbing in strength, forcing life back into his body. His bones seemed to groan and crack, bones that stuck out like the ribs of a starving dog.

Father motioned: *Come near.* His hand touched mine, his fingers hot from fever. Before, his skin had been cold.

His lips mouthed a simple request: "Sing."

I could not sing. Ashamed, I turned my face away. I shut my eyes. Outside, people were shouting, children crying. Everyone fleeing, running from our village, away from the sea where the sky had turned blood red. My sister sat watching, waiting.

Father's hand touched mine. "Sing, my son."

His touch, the sound of his voice ... my father had returned. He had defeated war.

I sang. Slowly his breathing relaxed. His arms ceased trembling. I sang, whispering in his ear, sometimes making no sound at all, watching his face, watching the tight lines soften. Breath by breath, my father's face relaxed. I sang the songs of our dances, warrior hymns, chants of the navigators. I sang of the sea that gives life and takes it, of our journey away from home and of our return. I sang to my father. I thought he was healing. I did not understand that he was dying.

The ground shook. The air smelled black with flames, oil, and gasoline. Our island was burning. But the bombs and fire had not come to our village yet. We had time before we must leave. The rain continued falling. Taeyo cried out. My sister murmured soft sounds, comforting words.

My mother sat next to me, her lips mouthing first the prayers of the rosary and then the chants of our ancestors. My father struggled to sit up. "Joseph, tell her."

My mother looked at me.

I shook my head.

My mother stroked my father's head. "You are home. You are safe. Rest."

Again he struggled to sit up. "Ignacio, run!"

My sister's eyes met Father's.

His eyes seemed to clear, to focus on my sister's face. "Anna Maria."

His eyes clouded with tears. "Ignacio ... is gone."

My sister stood, slipped outside, and ran to the sea. I heard her screams, her terrible keening pouring grief and fear across the water. Cries I shall never forget.

I stood to go after her.

My mother spoke. "No, Joseph, let her be. She cries her pain. She cries so her husband might find his way back. She cries to our ancestors to bring him home."

Father trembled. His breathing became more fitful. He called for my mother, "Rufina! Rufina Maria." She was holding him, offering him water, cooling his head with wet cloths. But he could not see her.

Finally his breathing calmed, became shallow, slower, and then he slept. He looked again like my father, the father I remembered. The father with whom I had danced and hunted turtle. His eyes flickered opened and met mine. "Take them to the cave."

I nodded so he would not argue. But I would not leave without my father.

His eyes closed. His lips parted slightly, repeating my mother's name. Tears slipped from his eyes. Bending near his face, my lips next to his ear, I sang. Over and over, stronger and stronger until his tears stopped flowing.

Curled up close to my father, my head next to his like a child's, I sang.

The ground shook again and again as if the sea had swelled into a giant wave that curled and crashed over our home. I did not realize I was dreaming. I was swimming through the swirling surf, struggling to reach my father. More waves swept him farther and farther away. A terrible roar filled my ears as I tumbled over and over. The water exploded. I woke shaking and confused.

My father did not move. I touched his forehead. It felt cool, almost cold. I stared at his chest but could not tell what was real and what I wanted to see. Prayed to see. I held his hand in mine. It was cold. It was not my father's hand.

My father was dead.

I screamed at the sky, the sea, at war. No! If I had kept singing ... he would still be alive. My father would still be alive.

The sky glowed after each explosion. Orange. Red. Burning. All around me the world was burning. My father was dead.

Night gave way to dawn. A dawn stinking of war, trembling with war.

I faced the sea but could not hear its voice. War split the air, pierced my ears with its screams. Smoke stained the horizon, curling around our village like the tentacles of some hideous monster.

From the ridge behind us, Japanese guns spewed fire

and smoke at the ships along the reef. Returning shells burst above our heads. Would the enemy come here and attack our village? The Japanese would fight back. But we would be scattered like minnows with no place to hide. We would be the little fish caught in the middle—caught between the hills and the ocean—between the Japanese and Americans. Caught in the crossfire. My father had understood. *Go to the cave. Hide. Wait.*

A low keening, my mother's cries mixed with prayers, pulled me back—to now, to my family. Mother was preparing my father's body for burial. She worked slowly, carefully, as if the war did not exist. She washed him and rubbed his skin with coconut oil perfumed with sweet ylang-ylang blossoms. Their fragrance would protect him from the dark spirits that would try to steal his soul. His body must be brought to the sea, to a sacred place. There the outgoing current would carry him over the reef to the ocean. There our ancestors would welcome him. There he could rest.

But who would carry him? Women were not allowed, not even his wife or daughter. Ignacio was gone. Everyone—uncles, nephews, and brothers—gone.

The rain continued falling, harder and harder. The rain was saying, *yes, I must do this. I must carry my father to the sea.* But I needed help. Then I would lead my family to safety as I had promised. To the cave. First I must carry my father home.

•

"Kento!"

I banged louder. "Kento, are you still here?"

The door opened a crack. "Is that really you, Joseph?" Kento peered out. "What are you doing here? Are you crazy? Soldiers—" He glanced behind me and pulled me inside.

I stood wet with sweat and rain. I gulped in deep breaths before I could finally blurt out, "Will you help me?"

Kento locked the door. Behind him, in the darkness of the unlit room a match flared and a candle was lit. The faces of his mother and sister stared back. I had not seen Kento's mother for a long time. After she married Kento's father, Tanaka-san, "the Japanese," she had lived apart from us.

Kento cleared his throat. "Joseph, we are leaving, soon. Tonight, to hide." Kento glanced at his mother, who nodded. "Joseph, my parents have urged me to ask again. Come with us. We will have food, water, protection—a safe place."

I bowed. "You are very generous. But—"

Ako shook her head. "Kento, tell him! Tell him the caves are not safe."

Kento raised his hand and signaled Ako to hush. "Our father sent word. Friends will take us—all of us—to safety. Don't go to the caves, Joseph. Come with us."

"Please, Joseph, don't go there!" Ako pleaded.

Kento nodded to Ako. "Leave, little sister. Now, please.

Joseph and I must—"

"No! I—" But their mother took Ako by the hand, and hurried them both from the room.

"Joseph, fighting is fierce in the south. The Americans are pushing north. Already they have taken Garapan." Kento swallowed. "Our soldiers will stop them ... soon, I'm sure, before they can attack here. Later, when your father returns—"

"My father is dead."

"Dead?"

I didn't know I was shouting. "Your people have done this!"

"My people?"

"Your people, the Japanese, they killed my father."

Our eyes locked. "Joseph, I am sorry. Forgive me for my rudeness." He bowed very low. I turned to leave.

Ako crept back in. She whispered, "My heart is sad for you, Joseph. Come with us."

I looked at her, so young, so brave.

"Joseph, you asked for help. What can we do? How can we help you?"

"I must carry my father to the sea, to Sa'dog Tasi."

"But Joseph—"

"My father came home." I met Kento's gaze. "I am his son."

Kento stared at me. "You are going to Sa'dog Tasi? Tonight? That would be suicide! American ships are bombing the beaches. Planes—"

"I am Rafalawash, Rapaganor, descendant of the navigators. My father's son." I met Kento's eyes with my own. "Will you help me?"

"Joseph." Kento stared at the floor. "I promised my father to stay with my family. I must keep that promise."

No one spoke. No one moved.

"Kento, I must carry my father to the sea. I cannot carry my father alone."

Kento did not look up. "I am sorry, Joseph, I cannot help you."

"You have turned your back on us. We are no longer of the same clan. You have become ... *Japanese*."

I ran from his house.

I wrapped my father's body in our most valuable mat, woven long ago by my own mother's mother, who had pounded long leaves of pandanus into fine thin threads and woven them to make this sacred mat, soft as a silk shawl. I stared at it and then at my mother, saw the pain on her face, and looked away.

My mother tied a burial cloth, a long red sash, around my waist. All was ready. I looked at the burial mat but did not voice my fear. Without help, I doubted I could carry him to the sea, to Sa'dog Tasi, the beginning of his spirit path. I reached down and lifted the mat. My legs were shaking. I held my father. I took a first step, stumbled, shifted the weight for better balance, then left. I walked without stopping, through the mud, through the gray rain, through the dark, except when an explosion lit the world—red, orange, yellow—for an instant ... until darkness returned.

The rain fell harder. I stayed away from the road, moving slowly. Each step meant pulling free from the mud, finding a secure place to step, keeping the mat balanced. At the river I would need to find the sharp curve where it deepened, where the current was strong. *See the place in your mind, Joseph. See it, and you will find it.*

Fireballs whistled across the sky, sometimes exploding over the sea, sometimes closer, overhead. With each bright pop I closed my eyes, afraid to breathe until finally the shell exploded—someplace far enough away— where it didn't blow us up. Then I took another step.

The rain poured even harder, sometimes like a waterfall. I could barely see, but I was afraid to wipe my eyes. My father felt heavy, cumbersome, and I was ashamed of wanting to quit. Ashamed again that I had stopped singing, had fallen asleep.

The shells from the ships fell closer, shaking the earth with each explosion. Along the hillsides, Japanese guns boomed back in reply. My arms grew numb. I no longer felt fear or grief or even the rain. As if I had left my body, I watched a mud-covered boy stumble through a waterfall of rain that fell on his head, down his back, and over his precious cargo.

Finally, I could hear the roar of rushing water amid explosions and thundering rain. I had made it to the river. I stepped in knee-deep water and began to slide. A board slammed into my legs. My knees buckled. A thick plank swirled by, spinning like a giant paddle. The current washed against me, pulling me deeper.

I caught the edge of the plank, steadied one side, and laid the mat on top. I tied it with the red cloth as the river grabbed and pushed. I chanted a few phrases of prayer: *Ancestors, come. Welcome my father, greet him.*

A high whistle screamed. Light burst behind my eyes and filled my head with pain. The river blew up, covering my face with mud and gravel. Water knocked me over and swirled me around. My father was gone.

Anna Maria stood outside our house, soaked, as water dripped down her face. She didn't seem to notice. "We must find Ignacio."

"We will," I lied. She did not ask about Father. I wanted to collapse, to fall asleep and not wake up. "Come inside, Anna Maria. It's dangerous out here."

She stared straight through me. "He will come home. He will look for me here." Rockets shrieked overhead. Explosions shook the earth. My eyes would no longer focus. I could hardly see what was real and what I feared.

My mother gently took my sister's hand, wrapped her in a shawl, and pulled her back inside. Taeyo was ready to be carried. Mother handed me our sleeping mats, then reached up into the rafters. She took down my father's dancing stick, pressed it to her chest, and placed it in my hands.

"Your father wanted you to have this. He is pleased with his son." Our eyes met for an instant.

I swallowed hard, turned away. One last time, I looked around the small room.

"All is ready." I picked up Taeyo. "Let me carry you on my back. Here, hold onto my shoulders." We walked out the door and left our home.

See it in your mind.

I could see nothing.

We stayed single file as we left our deserted village. The rain had stopped. The air stank of singed earth and burnt trees. My eyes soon stung from the acrid smell of explosives. To the south the horizon was a smudge of smoke and bursts of fire. The north was nothing but inky black. I wanted to stare at the sea, to hold its image in my mind. I looked up at the dark hillside on my right where we must soon climb. Brief bursts of rockets lit up patches of cliff and jungle, then *poof*, gone. Another explosion shook the ground.

We walked on—along the beach and then up the steep hillside, through the brush, always careful to stay in the tall grass as Father had done. First we must reach the ravine. My mother followed close behind, whispering the rosary or praying to our ancestors and always encouraging my sister, calming Taeyo when he cried.

Another explosion; it hit so close we felt a wave of heat. Taeyo called out for his father. My sister stopped and stared at the darkness that was the sea.

"Anna Maria, hurry." I tried to encourage her.

"Ignacio will search along the beach. He knows where to find me, where I wait for him."

I looked at my mother. "Tell her to hurry."

"She looks for her husband."

I hesitated, set Taeyo down on a boulder, and took my sister by the shoulders so we were face to face. Such touching of brother to sister was forbidden, unless ... unless her life was threatened. "Anna Maria, listen to me. We must keep walking. Ignacio wants his son to live. His new child—"

"His son to live? But Ignacio is looking for me."

"Anna Maria, when the fighting stops, I will bring you here, back home, back to the sea."

Her eyes searched mine. "Back here to the sea? You promise?"

I gripped my father's dancing stick. "I promise."

I remember the rain, the burning orange sky, and my bare feet slipping in the mud and stumbling on the sharp rocks. I remember my mother whispering her prayers, calming little Taeyo, and my sister following, head down, never speaking.

I remember darkness, rain splashing, as we huddled under trees, resting, listening. My mother patting my sister's hand, repeating her prayers, her lips moving, making no sound. *Holy Mary, Mother of God, pray for us* ...

I remember the rhythm of the dance singing in my head as we walked through the night, climbing, stopping to breathe and to pull my sister up when she fell, glancing back to see that my mother followed, helping them up the steepest parts.

We came to the top of the ravine. Here is where Father had said, *See it, Joseph. See it in your mind, and you will find it.*

I closed my eyes. In the darkness I could see.

戦争 WAR

Moonlight
Shines silver
Across breadfruit leaves,
Broken shards of light,
Broken dreams,
Broken.

The cave was farther than I remembered. And colder. The floor was slick with the ooze of dung and dust mixed with condensation. Water clung along the ceiling and dripped everywhere, on my head, my back, my arms. "Stop!" I wanted to scream. I could not imagine that soon I would long to hear the sound of water, to taste even one drop.

We were all cold, tired beyond feeling anything, even fear. Mother spread the sleeping mats across the damp, rocky floor. Taeyo curled up, still shivering, and immediately fell asleep. Anna Maria wrapped herself around him, warming him with her own body. Soon his shaking stopped and his body relaxed.

I checked the supplies. Everything was stacked exactly as before. That seemed a lifetime ago. Why had Ako warned us not to come here? Where was she hiding? Was she safe?

I sat near the entrance; my mother sat in the back,

near Anna Maria and Taeyo. Her lips continued to mouth words of prayer. I didn't realize I had dozed off until I awoke abruptly, shaking, startled by the roar of a plane followed by the sputter of machine guns. Taeyo cried out in his sleep. Anna Maria held him, massaged his wounded leg, whispered a song about brave young warriors. I dozed again until awakened by another explosion so near that the whole cave shook. Gravel and dust fell from the ceiling, clattered around us. A lone rat gnawed at a cane stalk, unperturbed by the sounds of gunfire or our presence. I threw a stick. *Get out!* The stick clacked against a rock and I saw again the searchlights, the pool of silver blood, the beach. Kento. We had been so eager to become warriors.

The rain continued, grew into a downpour.

"Good," my mother said.

Startled, I stared at her.

"Our footprints have been washed away. We are safe."

"Safe?" I did not know what to say.

"Joseph, we have only a few herbs for Tacyo's wound. We must use some of the water to keep it clean. Any infection would be dangerous."

Several days and nights passed. What was real and not real became a blur. The air turned hot and the cave soon stank of bat dung, rat droppings, and our own wastes, thinly covered in the shallow pit at the back of the cave. Finally the rain stopped, and rays of sunshine pierced through the canopy of leaves that curtained the cave's entrance. The warmth felt wonderful and I began to think, yes, we had made it to the cave, we were safe. Maybe the fighting would end soon, we would return home and find Ignacio. Maybe Taeyo's wound would heal quickly.

The sounds from the fighting grew louder, closer. I moved our mats farther from the entrance, safe from stray bullets. In one area, I could almost stand upright. I walked back and forth, touching every rock and crevice. I couldn't stop moving. I counted the coconuts, restacked them along the back wall, recounted. The gourds and bottles of water seemed too close to the entrance. I moved them. Shook my head, recounted, moved them again.

Anna Maria left Taeyo resting next to our mother and sat at the cave's mouth, near the ledge, gazing toward the sea.

"Move back," I urged. "You'll be seen. Or shot."

She would not answer and seldom moved except to care for Taeyo. She offered him chunks of soft coconut and the cooked breadfruit we had brought. After refusing food for several days, Taeyo was hungry, always hungry, a good sign, but his questioning voice was too loud. What if soldiers heard him? The Japanese threw grenades and sputtered bullets from their machine guns. The Americans ate children.

More days and nights passed, a blur of heat, explosions, gunfire, splashes of blinding light from rockets. No one spoke. We each sat alone, my mother and Taeyo in the middle of the cave, my sister at the front. I fought to stay awake. Sleep meant nightmares of being pulled down into the black ocean, my father's hand just out of reach, Kento disappearing.

More hot days and nights. The shelling had stopped, but gunfire continued and crept closer each day.

I recounted the coconuts, the bottles and gourds of water. Now, day ten, the stacks of supplies had dwindled. Soon they would be gone. I could not think, my mind would not follow one path. In frustration I restacked the stalks of cane. My fingers touched something smooth, something hard. My father's machete. Ever so carefully I picked it up as if it might shatter, sat down, held it in my arms, and cried.

My mother refused her share of food. "Anna Maria must eat for her child. Save the coconuts for her." My mother grew thin and listless. How long could we survive, hiding here like rats, not turtles? I opened two coconuts, one for my sister and one for Taeyo. His leg had healed and he could walk. He became restless. I smiled the first time he followed me like a shadow, pacing back and forth in the cave, arms behind his back, stooped over. Then I caught him throwing stones at the trunk of the breadfruit tree.

"Stop! Get back inside. Soldiers are out there, everywhere! You know they will shoot." I glared at my sister. "Why don't you stop him? He could get us all killed."

I shrunk from my words. Only last month, words spoken to me by my father.

The better Taeyo felt, the more he moved, the louder he spoke and the bigger his appetite. "I'm so hungry, Uncle Joe."

"One coconut a day, Taeyo. That's all. See how small the stack has become?" I didn't tell my nephew that for me, each day held only one small piece that I nibbled, chewed, and sucked out every bit of sweetness before I swallowed.

"Uncle Joe, can I climb down the tree?"

"No, don't go near that tree."

"Uncle Joe, let's do *something*."

His exaggerated frown made me smile. Yes, we all needed to do something. But what? Then I remembered. I pulled out Sensei's book. "Okay, come here." I opened to my favorite page. "'An ancient pond, A frog jumps in, The splash of water.'"

"What does that mean, Uncle Joe? 'Splash,' that's it?"

"Think, Taeyo, what does the splash begin? What cannot be stopped?"

"Ripples, Uncle Joe, everyone knows that."

"Further than we can know or see."

The book became our secret game. We studied the strange little poems, puzzles made of words. Each time I made Taeyo memorize one new kanji and practice writing it. I found a strong stick and sharpened it. He made rows of kanji; their lines scratched in the dirt floor soon crisscrossed our cave.

"Just like in the sand at the beach, Uncle Joe." We both grew quiet. Ako and Kento ... names we never spoke aloud. Where were they? Were they safe?

"See all the lines I made, Uncle Joe? They look like a fishing net. Let's catch a big fat shark."

I grinned, hoping his mother would notice, would turn her head away from her hopeless vigil. Anna Maria often seemed unaware of Taeyo, not answering his questions, not responding to his attempts to be silly. Silently she maintained her vigil at the cave's entrance.

"Uncle Joe?"

"Yes, Taeyo?"

"Where is my father?"

"I don't know, Taeyo."

"When will we see Ako again?"

"When? I can't promise exactly when, Taeyo, but when we do, she'll be so surprised at how many kanji you know."

Taeyo nodded and then poked at the dirt. He stared at his mother; she didn't seem to notice. He threw his writing stick against the wall and curled up into a tight ball.

That night I studied my little nephew's sleeping face. He was so young, so eager to explore, to learn, to live. *Wait like the turtle. How long, Father, how long?*

The heat continued. Hunger was a constant ache, but now, much worse, was our thirst. The need for water festered. All the bottles were empty. No matter how many times I recounted the gourds, the result was the same. We were almost out of water.

Dampness had dried to dust, which we breathed, swallowed, and choked on. The sun burned through the breadfruit leaves. Everything smelled dry and dead. Even the wind had deserted us.

We needed water. In my mind I saw the ravine, the grotto, the clear trickling stream. I had to get water. Again and again I crept to the entrance, knowing I needed to climb down, find the grotto, but a rattle of bullets would break the silence followed by moans and cries, so near! *Face your fear.* ... I could not.

Taeyo pushed away the book. Often he stayed curled up, refusing to speak, and even pushing away his share of food.

I sat near my sister. She did not seem to notice, not even to turn her head.

"Anna Maria?"

No response.

How could I awaken her? Taeyo needed her. "Anna Maria, I was remembering when Ignacio told me about how you two met."

Still nothing.

"... about *luus*."

She looked up. "Yes. Ignacio loves the telling of luus."

Taeyo heard his mother's voice, turned his head, and watched.

"Ignacio said you were the most beautiful of all."

A flicker of a smile flitted across her face.

"There was a full moon, like the one we will have soon."

My sister nodded.

"But the mothers didn't scold?"

"The mothers?" My sister looked at me. "The mothers? They sweetened our hair with coconut oil and ylang-ylang, hoping the love potion worked ... hoping the flowered *mwaar* would be captured by the most handsome one." She looked away, her head nodding.

"I walked slowly at first. My hair loose. Then I ran, how fast I ran."

"Ran, from what?"

"Oh, Joseph, that is the game, the chase. Who will run so fast to catch me? Only one, only Ignacio."

"And then the game is over?"

"Oh no, Joseph, it was just beginning. ..."

My face grew hot. I looked away.

"Open a coconut," Anna Maria said.

I looked at the small stack of coconuts, picked the best one, a green one, and whacked it open with the machete. My sister scooped out a handful of the sweet jelly inside, Taeyo's favorite. "My son, come here."

She placed the soft coconut in Taeyo's open hand, then asked, "The book Joseph reads to you, what does it say?"

"Important words."

"Show me."

Taeyo looked at me, eyebrows raised, asking. One quick raise of my own eyebrows and he scrambled to my mat, reached under, and showed his mother the last page we had read.

I stared at the clear, bright sky. Not one cloud. Think like a warrior, Joseph. *The grotto. Go there. Fill the gourds. Bring water home.* I shook my head. Home. This hole had become our home.

A branch snapped. Something moved below. Leaves brushed against branches. Rats? They scrambled constantly, everywhere, gnawing. *Please let it be rats.* Footsteps. Someone was scrambling up the hill. Coming closer.

Gunfire. Shouts. Someone—the sound of footsteps running through the undergrowth below us. More shots. Shrapnel zinged against the cliff.

Bullets ricocheted along the front of the cliff. I pushed my sister down and then rolled on top of Taeyo. More bullets splintered the rock above us.

Soldiers shouted and crashed through the bush. More gunshots. Rocks clattered and slid. Screaming pierced the air. Then light burst. Men moaned. Smoke drifted past the entrance, curling and twisting like a snake.

Don't cry, little one, don't cry, I prayed, I begged.

Taeyo did not move, did not cry.

My ears filled with their own ringing.

"Mother of God, pray for us, now and at the hour

of our death." My mother's lips moved in prayer, never making a sound; her body rocked back and forth.

My sister lay with her arms around her son. Her backbone was a sharp ridge along the curve of her back, her limbs were so thin, and her skin, rough with dust.

My sister, my mother, my nephew; they were barely more than dusty bones.

They needed water.

I waited until dark, blackened the machete blade with spit and dirt, and tied empty gourds to my waist.

See the grotto. Go to it. I eased myself down the tree, branch by branch, listening.

My toes touched the ground. To feel earth was wonderful—to touch green leaves, a blossom, soft soil. I walked without having to stoop, without a ceiling of stone over my head, without walls. Everything smelled fresh, green and alive!

I hurried straight down the steep slope, listening for voices or footsteps. My ears became my eyes. Gunfire was constant. Rockets whistled overhead. Each time their high-pitched scream began, I stopped until I heard the explosion, felt the blast of light, and then I breathed out, knowing this time I was safe.

I stumbled over something. A branch? A fallen tree? The smell of burnt flesh was strong. I felt something soft. An arm, a soldier's body. I felt for his canteen. My fingers touched cold flesh. Vomit burned in my throat. I turned and pushed through the branches. I didn't care who heard me. *Shoot me. But I must find water. My family needs water.*

I stumbled into the ravine. The ravine! *Joseph,* Father had warned, *stay lower. Don't stop. Hurry.* How did I miss the grotto? I climbed back up, back to the top of the ravine where the paths began. I continued straight uphill. If I could get close to the grotto, I would smell the moist cool air—water. Others would, too. Others with rifles.

I stopped, breathing hard but listening. Yes, I could hear it. A whisper of water trickled over rock. I pushed through a curtain of vine and my fingers felt soft, moist moss. I pressed my tongue against the moss, tasted the water as it filled my mouth, swallowing again and again. I closed my eyes, rested. My father was right, water is life.

I scraped the dried, caked mud. The flow grew stronger. One by one I filled the gourds and set them on the ground. My family would have water. I gave thanks to the spirits, "Help me return and ... help Kento, Ako, all the people of our clan, and Ignacio. May no one suffer tonight from thirst."

I drank again and let water run down my chin and chest. I splashed my face and rubbed my eyes. I could see their faces—Ako's pouting mouth and Kento's frown. Did he still stare at the stars and the moon?

Something moved through the bushes. I froze, listening. Slow, careful steps, one step and then one more. My hand touched the ground, and my fingers gripped the machete.

"Joseph?"

I froze. Who had spoken my name? My father? Who else? Was I crazy? I did not trust my ears, my eyes, not even my mind.

"Joseph?"

I lifted the machete, ready to strike. "Who are you?"

"I've come as a friend, the one who hunts turtle but falls in the sea."

"Kento?" My throat was so dry that his name sounded like a bark.

A figure stepped into the thin shaft of moonlight and bowed.

"Kento, it's really you?"

"Joseph, it is me ... your friend."

Was this Kento or his ghost? The face staring at me was thin and pale, but the voice—it was Kento's voice. Still I did not move.

He bowed again. Yes, of course, even if Kento was dying, first he would bow. This was Kento standing in front of me. I wanted to weep.

"Joseph, I was afraid ... you are alive. ... You made it to the cave?"

"What are you doing here? How did you find this place?"

"Your father told me."

"My father?"

"He came to our house before he left for the airfield. He brought me here and said to tell no one. Not even you." Kento cleared his throat, took several breaths. "Your father knew that if the Japanese won, I could help you. But I would have to know how to find you."

"But he told me not to trust you. That you would choose your family ... and not ours." I remembered Kento's betrayal, his refusal to help. "My father was right."

"He knew defeat was possible. If the Japanese lost ... no one could imagine what would happen, no one, not your father or mine." Kento's voice softened. "Joseph, I am ashamed. I apologize, I failed you." Another bow. "Now I am the one asking for help."

"My help?"

"I must find the cliffs and go there, quickly. Where are they, how do I get there? Can you tell me?"

"The cliffs to the north? But why?"

"I went to find food. Last night. When I returned, Mother and Ako were gone."

"Gone?"

"We had heard of orders to march to the cliffs. Everyone. I thought they were rumors." Kento held his head in his hands. "The code of the samurai. Remember, Joseph, remember? Defeat ... dishonor ... death."

"Let the soldiers kill themselves."

"Joseph, you don't understand. Everyone!"

"Everyone?" I closed my eyes, refusing to believe what Kento was saying. "Everyone? Even children? Ako?"

"I should never have left them alone. But we were so hungry."

"They are being taken to the cliffs? The northern cliffs? Are you sure?"

"How do I get there? Joseph, tell me."

My father had warned me that the Japanese would sacrifice everything. But their own children?

"Joseph, please. Tell me how to get there."

Father had warned, *Stay away from this place. ... Never come here again.*

"Joseph, are you deaf? I need to find them *now*. Tell me how to get there. Please!"

"Kento, you will have to run, first uphill and then across the savannah. Do you have strength to run that far?"

"Yes. I don't know. I will."

"We will take this water to my family first. The cave is not far. I must tell them where we are going in case we don't return. Then we will head north, make our way through the trees, stay away from the path, until we reach the cliffs."

"You will go with me, Joseph?"

"I was there once, long ago." I picked up the gourds of water, tied them to my waist. "We will find them."

I do not remember how we crossed the ridge of the island without getting lost or shot. In my mind I saw the ragged wall of forbidden cliffs and heard my father's words: *Stay away.* I saw the precipice that plunged straight down, the place of lost spirits, of a moaning wind that never stopped. In my mind I saw my people marching. ... I saw

Ako, ribbons in her hair. Could we find her, and if we did, could we save her?

We ran, stumbling over splintered trees and bushes, pushing through twisted vines and thorny branches. We saw the burnt and bombed hillsides, climbed over black skeletons of trees, and fell over charred bodies of dogs, pigs, water buffalo ... and people. Bellies lay swollen, legs stiff, and eyes open, staring. I could not look at them. *Father, did you know this was war?*

The sun rose, and the jungle became an oven. We ran with sweat running down our faces, stinging our eyes; we ran until the burning in our lungs forced us to rest. When our chests stopped heaving and our legs stopped shaking, we ran again, always north, always higher, until we neared the cliffs.

By midday we reached the high, flat plateau—the savanna—and I wanted to turn around. Far ahead, helicopters circled, their engines roared, and machine guns popped. What if we were too late? Storm clouds were building high and dark over the distant ocean. Sweeps of rain blew toward us, like a smudge of gray skimming across the water. The wind pushed us back as dust blew in our eyes and smoke burned our throats. The clouds cooled the air and blocked the blistering sun, and rain poured down like a river. We opened our mouths and drank. But the wind never ceased, never relented, and soon it blew away what it had given. The clouds swept past and thinned, the sky lightened, and the rain stopped.

We pushed through the thick grass of the savanna and over muddy ashes where the grass had burned. We ran. We heard screams and shouts. Then in the distance, they appeared: an endless stream of people. Soldiers marched, children stumbled, mothers carried babies on their backs, and fathers held little ones in their arms. A girl held her little brother by the hand. Natives walked next to Japanese, women and children next to soldiers. War made no distinctions.

As we got closer, classmates appeared. Tomo! I saw my classmate, the quiet one whose fingers clicked the abacus beads faster than anyone. Next to him walked a white-haired grandfather, stooped and pale, holding Tomo by the hand as if he were a child. His grandfather carried a little girl, her black hair braided and tied with red ribbons. Ribbons. I had to find Ako.

Helicopters swooped overhead like giant buzzing flies. No Imperial red sun rose on their metallic sides. Americans! The men inside shouted words I did not understand. Their megaphones urged in Japanese: *Stop. Do not jump. We will not hurt you.* Slips of white paper fluttered to the ground. *We will not hurt you. Do not jump.* People stepped through the swirling papers as if they were falling leaves.

And then I saw Sensei, his tall thin figure walking forward. "No!" I screamed, but nothing came from my mouth. I saw him standing in front of our class and I heard again his words: *I have my duty. Take care of yourself. Your family, your people.*

Then what I saw, I could not believe. A mother with two children darted away from the stream of people marching toward the cliffs. She pulled one child behind her, the other she held. Gunfire. She slumped over, shot. Another soldier rushed over to her. He lifted his sword, one slash, then another. All three lay beheaded. Others pushed past the bodies, showed no reaction. They walked onward to the cliff.

"Joseph, what's wrong with you? Why are you standing there? We must find them *now!*" Kento screamed.

A volley of gunfire exploded between two groups of soldiers, Americans above in helicopters and Japanese not far from us. Startled, I shuddered, aware that Kento and I were in their crossfire.

I began running, yelling like a madman, "Ako! Ako-chan!"

We slipped between trees, screaming, calling. If we were seen, we would be shot. I didn't care. We kept running toward the cliff.

Ahead of us, families lined up in orderly rows. Mothers holding their babies stepped off the cliff edge, staring straight ahead. Children followed, one after another, leaped to their deaths. Last came fathers, running backwards, not knowing which step would be their last.

I stared, unable to move, unable to utter a sound. I couldn't look away. One after another, a child, a mother, a father, stepped off the cliff.

Kento saw her first. She walked calmly, hand in hand

with their mother, looking as fragile as a porcelain doll in a glass case.

"Ako!" Kento screamed.

Ako turned and looked around, as if startled from sleep.

"Ako! Mother! Stop!" Kento screamed and ran toward them.

Ako's eyes grew round. She tugged hard on her mother's hand and pointed. Kento pushed through the chaos of marching people.

Three young women bolted from the cliff and ran toward a tangle of trees on the far slope. Helicopters swooped over them. Japanese soldiers fired, first at the women, then at the helicopters. People ran in all directions, terrified of both the soldiers and the whining blades that whipped dirt and mud. One woman screamed, ran toward the woods, fell, crawled between rocks and boulders, and fell again. A soldier followed her. As he bent over her sprawled body, my heart pleaded, *No, leave her alone.* The soldier helped her up and then watched as she continued toward the trees to hide, to disappear into safety.

This was our chance. We too must disappear. "Kento, Ako, now!" I shouted and waved my arms. "Run to the rocks, here, over here!"

Ako grabbed her mother's arm and dodged between people, toward her brother. I ran to them, calling in our native language. "Come, Auntie! We are going home.

Run this way. We are going home."

People pushed past. An old lady fell down. A soldier shot her in the head. The man next to her began to cry and knelt beside her. Someone pushed by and knocked me over. I scrambled back up, ran to catch up with the others, and grabbed my aunt's arm. "Follow me, we'll hide behind those rocks, we will be safe." I heard an order shouted and then another shot. I turned around.

Tomo stood at the cliff next to his grandfather and the little girl.

The grandfather reached down, picked up the little girl, kissed her forehead, kissed the red ribbons that danced in the wind. He hugged her close, her head tucked beneath his chin, took Tomo's hand, and stepped off the cliff.

"No!" I screamed.

Kento yanked at my arm. I held onto my aunt. Together we walked into the jungle, to hide, to safety. We huddled behind a pile of boulders while his mother rested, needing to breathe, gasping for air.

Endless shots—a cacophony of screams, shouts, gunfire, the roaring of helicopters and, still, the wind's unmerciful howling. I fell to my knees, covered my ears with my hands, and cried. The people flowed on and on like a river. *Sa'dog tasi* ... river to the sea. *My people ... my people.*

希望と幸せ HOPE

Black butterfly,
Sit on my ears, my lips,
My fingertips.
Whisper.

"See that spider web, Joseph? See how it shimmers in the light?"

I didn't look up. I sat hunched over, arms around my legs.

"Please look, just once. It's the biggest web I've ever seen."

The web stretched across several branches of the breadfruit tree right outside the cave. "You're right, Ako. It is big. But scoot back. Remember, I said never go past this line."

"Right in the middle is the spider, like a jewel, gold and green."

Our cave was crowded. Hot and smelly. We had little food. Not enough water.

"I've never been in a cave before. It's creepy." Ako wrinkled up her nose. "It sure does smell."

"Ako, stay back from the entrance." She was stubborn and interested in everything. Even after all that had happened.

I spoke sharply. "Stay back. Sit by your mother. Whisper. Don't talk so loud."

"You're talking louder than me." She grinned. "Spiders live outside. I like to sit out here near Anna Maria and Taeyo. Anyway, it doesn't smell out here."

"Stay back. That's an order."

Ako shook her head, and her long braids whipped back and forth. I saw again the cliff, the grandfather ... red ribbons. Nausea swept through me.

"Spiders are lucky, Joseph. Imagine bathing in raindrops."

"And eating bugs? How lucky is that?"

"Oh, Joseph, you're so grumpy! Aren't you glad we're here? Look. Black butterflies! Two of them." She pointed at the leaves outside. She looked at me, eyebrows raised. "Joseph, if butterflies can survive, so can we." She was inching closer to the front.

"Get back!"

"When I see butterflies, I *feel* butterflies inside me. Wouldn't it be wonderful to fly!"

I had to smile. "You're right, Ako. They are lovely."

We watched their wings fluttering, blue-black iridescence, and each wing was dotted with one yellow circle. The pair flew between the breadfruit leaves, tasting the tiny clusters of blossoms. Ako watched with such intensity, such focus.

"Please move back, Ako."

"Come here, Joseph," Kento called from inside the cave.

He sat cross-legged in a place where he had scraped the dirt flat and patted it smooth. He had scratched several kanji in the dust. He handed me his stick. "Your turn."

"I've forgotten."

"Try."

I copied a few lines, then threw the stick down. Waiting was killing us as surely as the thirst and hunger.

"Try again." Kento made me draw the lines until I got each one exactly right and in the correct order.

Ako snatched the writing stick and wrote:

Rain begins morning,
Mist cools my skin.
Teardrops
Whisper
And fall.

"Father taught me that poem. When I see him, I'll show him how much I've learned. I will, Joseph." I was caught by the sadness in her voice.

Kento nodded. "See, Joseph, writing is like making a canoe."

"Kento, moon-man, you talk riddles."

"Joseph, if trees can become canoes, words can become poems. Poems fly us far from here."

"I'd rather carve a canoe."

"Words can take us—"

"To the moon? Is that how you're going to get there? With words?"

"Someday I will, Joseph."

"You can. You are Japanese!" I threw down the stick.

Kento swept his stick across the dirt. Gone! Canoe and moon were nothing but a pile of dirt.

I moved to the back of the cave, near my sister. Taeyo stirred and opened his eyes.

"What's wrong, Uncle Joe? Your face is one big frown."

"Go back to sleep, Taeyo."

I wanted to hit, to fight, to *do* something. When would this waiting end? And then what?

Taeyo gave me a poke. "Hey, stop that," I growled. He grinned and held up my book.

"Read to me, Uncle Joe." Taeyo opened Sensei's book to his favorite page. How many times had we read that same poem? How many times had he asked the same questions?

Kori nigaku enso ga nodo o uruoseri ...

Bitter-tasting ice—
Just enough to wet the throat
Of a sewer rat.

"What is ice, Uncle Joe?"

"I don't know, Taeyo."

"You said your teacher explained it. Remember?"

"My teacher explained many things I did not understand."

"What is a sewer, Uncle Joe?"

"What do you think it is?

"Where rats live? A cave? Like here?"

My sister must have been listening. She smiled at her son, and I remembered how she used to smile at all of us, at Ignacio, how her eyes sparkled that night she danced alongside our mother. The two of them strutting in front of the men, so funny, dancing the saucy steps of the women's courting dance. Now, again, after all that had happened, my sister smiled.

Maybe Ako was right, maybe we could survive.

Warm light from the evening sun shimmered on the branches outside. Something flittered from blossom to blossom. The butterflies were back.

I sat next to Kento. "I'm sorry. I don't know what's wrong with me. I ..."

"War makes us crazy, Joseph."

"I'm sick of hiding."

"The fighting can't last much longer."

"And then what? When I try to sleep, Kento, I see the cliffs. I can't get them out of my head."

"Joseph, the cliffs are done. Focus, like a warrior. Use your mind, your strongest weapon."

"Your samurai warriors killed themselves."

"Stop going backwards, Joseph, stop." He picked

up a stick, jabbed it in the dirt. "Listen to me, Joseph. Think about rain. Taste it, hear it falling. Focus." Kento scratched long lines of kanji in the dirt:

Surf's
> *Edges sharpen,*
> *White into*
> *Indigo, folds,*
> *Leaps*
> *Free.*

"Soon *we* will be free, Joseph."

I shook my head. "If the Americans win, what will happen to us?"

"The Americans *are* winning."

I looked out past the cave, closed my eyes, and struggled to see the ocean. First I heard it, smelled the salty air. I sat in my canoe as I had as a child, my father sat in the back. I paddled away from shore, felt the slap of the water and the splash of the sea, and tasted salt on my tongue.

Someone shook me.

"Uncle Joe, when will we go home? Maybe my father is waiting. I want to go home."

"Soon, Taeyo, soon."

"You promise? But you make so many promises."

"Come here. Yes, here beside me. Remember when Father taught us how to dance, how to fly."

"Uncle Joe, really? Fly?"

"Taeyo, listen. Here." I tapped my chest. "Do you remember the story of the dance?" I walked my fingers up his arm; he brushed them away. "It came in a dream ... in the darkness of the night."

Taeyo pressed his hands over his ears.

"Okay, little one, but someday we will tell it again. We will sit on the shore and wiggle our toes in the waves. Someday." I wrapped my arms around my little nephew, held him close, let him cry, and then slept a long dreamless sleep.

Before I opened my eyes, I could smell the rain. A hush spread through the trees. Not even a gecko chirped or a kingfisher squawked. All became still.

The fronds of the tallest palms trembled. Bamboo stalks clattered. Even the broad breadfruit leaves began to sway in the wind, back and forth, like giant green hands begging for water.

In the distance, water splashed. I could hear raindrops falling on leaves, branches, and rocks.

My mother sat up, and Kento's mother next to her. Anna Maria raised her head and looked around. I crawled to the entrance and searched the night sky. No stars. Only black, beautiful storm clouds. Raindrops fell on my face, first just a few, then more and more. I stuck out my tongue.

"Rain! It really is raining. Come and drink it."

The rain stopped. We waited, praying and watching

as another gray curtain blew closer, splashing louder until rain thundered down like a waterfall. We became silly schoolchildren, our heads tilted back, our tongues out. We hugged each other, laughing, as wet, wonderful rain poured down. We clapped and sang and made cups with our hands, caught raindrops, and drank handful after handful.

"The gourds, the bottles! Get them. Fill them up."

Everyone but Anna Maria ran to the back of the cave. She stood at the edge of the opening. She stood with her hands held up to the wet sky and let the rain splash her face. Wonderful cool water splashed everywhere.

I watched her. Kento was counting the empty bottles and gourds and dividing them up.

"Help me, Joseph, we'll fill every single one with water!"

I stepped back into the cave but stopped. Everything stopped. The rapid *pop-pop-pop* of gunfire pierced the air. "Get down. Everyone, get down." I pushed Ako down into the dirt.

A volley of bullets pitted the rock, spewed metal and gravel. A shrill whistle and then a blast shook our world. A blinding light exploded behind my sister. The trunk of the breadfruit tree shattered. The entire cave shuddered.

And then silence.

The stink of sulfur and scorched rock filled the cave. More gunfire sounded, this time from a distance. A wet breeze blew through the broken branches. Rain continued to fall.

Afraid to my very core, I listened.

Ako cried behind me. Her head was buried in her mother's lap. Kento grabbed my arm and held on tight. My mother rocked Taeyo back and forth, her lips again moving silently in prayer ... *and at the hour of our death, pray for us.*

I scrambled to my sister, who lay where she had fallen. Blood pooled in the mud around her head. Dark red oozed around her beautiful black hair. I stared.

Please be alive.

My mother took my sister in her arms, carried Anna Maria inside, and carefully laid her on a mat.

"Don't go!" Kento pleaded.

"Anna Maria's wounds are deep. She is weak. Medicine and herbs are needed to stop the bleeding." My mother repeated to Kento what she had already said to me.

Kento's mother had washed and cleaned my sister's wounds. One bullet had pierced her neck, another had punctured her side.

Ako stared from the back of the cave and hugged herself to hide the trembling. My aunt described what was needed: leaves from the shore vines, gathered at dawn when the leaves are still cool and damp with dew. I should pick them when their healing strength is strongest and bring the fresh leaves to make a poultice to cover the wounds. This and fresh green coconuts so their milk would give my sister strength to heal. I picked up Father's machete and blackened the blade.

"Joseph, listen to me," Kento pleaded. "Wait until morning. Now is too dangerous."

"I cannot let my sister die."

Around my waist I knotted a strip of cloth to fill with leaves. "Kento, make my mother drink, even if she refuses. Her mind is sometimes confused. Keep Ako away from the ledge. And Taeyo ... read to him. It quiets him." We looked at each other. Kento bowed. I bowed back.

"Take care of our families, my friend. Let Ako sit next to Anna Maria. Her chatter soothes her." I placed my hands on Kento's shoulders. "I should be back before tomorrow night."

"Joseph!" Ako ran over, pulled loose one of her hair ribbons and looped it around my wrist. "This will keep you safe."

"Thank you, little warrior."

I looked around our crowded cave, not wanting to leave. I bowed, hurried to the ledge, and climbed down the splintered tree until once again my feet touched the ground. I did not stop or look back.

At the grotto, I rested briefly and drank. Memories flowed with the water: I saw my sister's face when Ignacio returned from fishing, the pride in her eyes and mischief in her smile. I heard my father's voice when he whispered that Ignacio was gone. I saw the longing and hope in my sister's eyes as she stared out from the cave.

I followed the ravine and stayed low. Swaths of ground were singed black, smoking in the ghostly light of the moon. I stopped to stare at the butchery: bodies blown apart, overturned jeeps, bloated soldiers. I picked my way around, then ran the last part, down the long, steep slope. Our island was rotting with death.

I heard the surf before I could see it, the roar from the tide rushing in and crashing. My father was right: The sea survives. I ran to the shore and waded in. The ocean's skin rippled alive as light spread across the waves. Slips of white birds soared high overhead, winging toward deeper ocean. They had survived.

Searching, I picked my way along the shore. Vines once covered this beach. When we were children, Kento and I had picked armfuls of vines and seaweed and then chased each other, teasing and piling them on ourselves until we smelled of sea and fish.

A terrible buzzing stopped me. I followed the sound and discovered a tiny marsh. Backwash had piled bloated bodies ashore in tangled heaps. Black flies crawled everywhere. I ran, seeing soldiers with bodies swollen like dead fish and empty eyes that stared upward. I fell to my knees and vomited, then covered my face.

I held my knees and rocked, the waves rolled in, crashed along the shore, and slipped out.

I had to cleanse myself of the rot and stench. I ran into the waves, then pulled and kicked through the water. Light danced around me. Below me was darkness. *Remember the dance, and you will know* ... know what, Father?

I had promised.

I returned to the shore and walked away from the death and flies. I searched until I found vines that were still alive and green with leaves. I fingered Ako's ribbon and gave thanks to our ancestors. Then I sat and rested, listening to the endless singing of the sea, watching the sunlight dance on the waves.

Plumes of smoke curled above the north end of the island where the cliffs lay. The southern horizon was clear. Was it over? A plane buzzed low over the reef. On its side was a large white star, not the red circle of Japan. Would the Americans kill us all?

Though the sun was bright overhead, I could not wait. I climbed back to the grotto, gulped water, then slapped mud over my head, arms, and body. The mud soothed the scratches and cooled my burning skin. Maybe when I got to the cave, Ako would laugh and tease, "Mud man!"

Again I drank, swallowing slowly, staring at the steep hill that rose before me, with its walls of bushes and vines. If only I could rest.

Something flickered in the bushes. My throat tightened. Then I smiled. A black butterfly. Two of them, dipping and fluttering like the pair outside the cave. I watched, my eyes holding onto them even after they were gone. *I will keep my promise.*

I never heard the soldier.

Cold metal pressed against the back of my head. I closed my eyes and waited. How strange! I was no longer in my body but a spectator, watching. Would I hear the explosion or feel the bullet shatter my skull?

My entire body began to shake, and I could not make it stop. A firm hand grabbed my shoulder and turned me around. I looked up at a dusty face with black lines under the eyes, a face half-hidden by a helmet. A face with blue eyes.

An American soldier, a man who eats children. Would he hit me across the face or just pull the trigger? I didn't want to die. Who would bring Anna Maria these herbs? The bleeding had to stop; her wound needed to heal. Who would tell Taeyo the story of the dance? Who would sit with Ako and watch the butterflies?

I didn't want to die.

I stared at the blue eyes. Blue like the sea. *I want my family to live.*

He spoke words I did not understand and then reached into his pack and pulled out a small book with kanji on the cover. He opened it and pointed: *Are you hungry?*

I tried to answer. My body would not stop shaking. What kind of a warrior was I? I stared at his rifle.

He set his rifle down and took something out of his pack. He broke it in half, put one piece in his mouth. "*Daijobu desu*, it is okay. It is safe." He handed me the other half. Sweetness filled my mouth. Chocolate! Ako had once brought this strange food to share with us at the cove. I swallowed, felt sick, and covered my face with my hands. What kind of warrior vomits in front of his enemy?

"*Tomodachi*, friend." He showed me his canteen, drank from it, and handed it to me. "Drink ... it is safe. I am a friend, *tomodachi*. Drink."

When the soldier took me by the arms to pull me up, my knees buckled. I almost fell. He pointed down the hill and motioned to walk that way.

I pulled back, shook my head, and sat down.

He sat next to me. My father had warned, *Trust no one*, but he had shown Kento the grotto. This soldier had food and water, and maybe medicine.

His blue eyes watched me. Again he pointed at his book. "Food." He pointed down the hill. "Many *tomodachi*, many friends, plenty food." He mimicked eating, and again he pointed and ordered. "*Ikimasho*. We must go." He took my arm and pulled. I twisted loose but fell backwards. I had so little strength.

He took out a thin leather envelope, opened it, and showed me a picture of a woman holding a little girl, then pointed to a different kanji in the book—*kasoku-ka*. He pointed to himself and then to the picture. "Family."

I understood.

A stranger came to our ancestor. In a dream ... our clan was dying.

What should I do?

"What do you believe, Joseph? Someday when you are lost in a darkness that you do not understand ... you will know."

What should I do?

Listen to the fire within.

I could hear nothing, not even the sea.

I stood up, held out my empty hands. *See, I have no weapons. I am harmless. Aim your rifle, shoot me ... or let me return to my family.*

Today I had seen flies feasting on war. I had seen butterflies ... black butterflies.

I stared at this soldier, at his strange blue eyes, a stranger, an enemy who took out a book, not a weapon, and pointed to a picture of his family.

I listened for an answer and heard my own.

I turned and walked uphill to my family.

The soldier followed.

治平 TO SEE, PEACE

After darkness
We see
What had been
Un-seeable.

My sister lay across the laps of my mother and aunt in the back seat of the jeep. She was wrapped in a soft blanket, and Taeyo sat huddled next to her. My mother cradled Anna Maria's bandaged head. Ako sat perched on one side, looking, pointing, or sometimes only staring. Kento sat between the two soldiers in the front seat, stiff and straight as he once sat in the canoe. Someday we would paddle back over the reef.

Once down the hillside, we skirted around our village, Tanapag, and then followed what was left of the coral road, pocked from bombs and explosions. We were being taken to a "camp" where they said there were already many natives. Was Ignacio waiting for us there? Kento's father? The soldiers said we would be given tents for shelter, food, clean water, and medicine for Anna Maria. They talked to us through a translator, a young Chamorro man from Guam who knew Japanese and already some English. They addressed him as Ranger. Whenever his eyes met mine, he nodded.

The jeep bumped along. I looked at Ako. Her lips whispered, "Butterflies."

Yes, we had survived.

The jeep stopped. We all lurched forward.

"Is there a problem?" I looked at the ranger, my heart already racing.

The ranger shook his head. "Just looking for a place to cross this river. It's running high from yesterday's rains."

The soldiers walked up and down the bank, searching out a shallow area where they could drive the jeep across. I whispered to my sister, "We are back. Look, Anna Maria, the ocean."

She tried to sit up but was too weak. My mother lifted her just enough so my sister could see the ocean.

"Ignacio," she whispered, then looked at me. Her eyes said everything.

"Yes, maybe we will find him."

My mother rewrapped the blanket and took my sister's hand in hers.

I climbed out of the jeep and stared at the place where Kento and I had met secretly after school ... long ago ... and where I had carried my father. Many of the bread-fruit and mango trees were gone, broken and ripped apart, but some were still standing.

Father, like the turtle, we waited.

A line of coconut palms swayed with the breeze,

chattering with the wind as if nothing had changed. I followed the river's bank to the shoreline and then stopped. The tide was changing. Surf crashed along the reef, leaping white and high.

Our ancestors were dancing—spinning, sweeping, flying.

The sea continues.

Our family had survived.

The ocean stretched out before me. I watched as waves washed over my bare feet.

This work of fiction is set on the island of Saipan during World War II, in the spring of 1944. It does not tell the story of a real-life Carolinian (Repagúnúworh/Rapaganor, Refaluwasch/Rafalawash), Chamorro or Japanese boy and his family. But the major events are true, and they represent the history of many families caught in the terrible crossfire of invasion and resistance. The Japanese defended the island almost to the last living soldier. Foreign workers from Korea and Okinawa were rounded up and exterminated. American forces bombarded relentlessly, attacking first the southern shores, and then advancing across the length of the island to the northern cliffs.

Many indigenous families tried to survive the invasion by hiding in caves located high along the steep, heavily wooded hillsides. Many were killed—sometimes outright, sometimes by sniper fire, sometimes by mistake. All suffered from terrible thirst and hunger. Young men and boys would sneak out at night to find food and water, often returning with nothing. Often they did not return at all.

When it became apparent to the Japanese that the American forces would prevail, all Japanese citizens, military and civilians—men, women, and children—were marched to the northern end of the island to a precipice that plummets straight down for more than 800 feet. Some were marched to Bonzai Cliff and forced to leap into the sea. Families lined up, youngest to oldest, walking backwards until they stepped, or were pushed, over the cliff's edge. From helicopters, American soldiers dropped leaflets and broadcast messages urging people not to jump but to surrender. These reassurances had little effect; hundreds leapt to their deaths. That precipice is now known as Suicide Cliff.

Families that were captured were taken to a refugee camp located in the area called Susupe. Native families (Rafalawash, Rapaganor, and Chamorros) were kept in an area separate from Japanese civilians and prisoners of war. For two years these families were confined within the camp until Liberation Day, July 4, 1946.

More than thirty thousand people died during the battles on Saipan and neighboring Tinian. Many others died caught in the crossfire on other islands of the western Pacific. From these captured islands Americans then made air strikes against Tokyo, Iwo Jima, Hiroshima, and Nagasaki. Island nations continued to suffer after the war because of the extent of deforestation, radioactive contamination, and destruction of natural plant and animal life.

Today, on these same islands, Asian and American tourists play on pristine white sand beaches in front of luxury hotels. The blood of the many lives lost has washed away. May the memory of their struggles and tragic deaths not wash away. May the courage of those who survived always be remembered.

Memorials along these suicide cliffs entreat:

Better to light one candle than curse the darkness.
May we live together in peace.

治平 TO SEE, PEACE

After darkness
We see
What had been
Un-seeable.

Suggestions for other books to read about young people and war, war in the Pacific arena, and related subjects:

Adam Bagdasarian: *Forgotten Fire,* the story of a young man who survives the Armenian holocaust in 1915.

Theodore Taylor: *The Bomb,* about the atomic bomb testing in the western Pacific, the Marshall and Bikini islands, following World War II.

Theodore Taylor: *The Cay,* a story of a boy's survival on an island in the Caribbean, following a World War II submarine attack.

Harry Mazer: *A Boy at War: A Novel of Pearl Harbor*
              A Boy No More
              The Last Mission
              Heroes Don't Run: A Novel of the Pacific War

Graham Salisbury: *Under the Blood-Red Sun*
                 House of the Red Fish
                 Eyes of the Emperor